UNTOUCHABLE

A NOVEL BY

KATE BRIAN

SIMON PULSE

New York London Toronto Sydney

SIMON PULSE
An imprint of Simon & Schuster Children's Publishing Division
1230 Avenue of the Americas, New York, NY 10020

Produced by Alloy Entertainment
151 West 26th Street, New York, NY 10001

Cover design by Julian Peploe
Book design by Amy Trombat
The text of this book was set in Filosofia.

Manufactured in the United States of America
First Simon Pulse edition December 2006

6 8 10 9 7 5

Library of Congress Control Number 2006929317

ISBN-13: 978-1-4169-1875-2
ISBN-10: 1-4169-1875-2

CHARADE

My first funeral. My first funeral was for the first guy to ever see me naked. This could not be right.

It wasn't for a grandparent or for a friend's elderly aunt with wrinkles so deep you could stash stuff in them, but for Thomas. Thomas Pearson. The first classmate I had met at Easton Academy. The first person who had made me feel semi-welcome. Gorgeous, mysterious, intense Thomas Pearson. The person I had lost my virginity to.

So many moments kept replaying themselves in my mind, and no matter what I did, I couldn't seem to make them stop. The moment Josh Hollis had rushed back through the fog to tell me that Thomas was dead. The moment I had found the note from Thomas telling me he was going to be all right, and how stupid I felt now to have believed it. The last moment I had seen Thomas, leaving my dorm room at Bradwell. It seemed like so long ago. I didn't even live there anymore. Thomas had never seen my new room at Billings. Now he never would. Because now he was lying cold and dead in a coffin. In the ground somewhere, in a coffin. The family had opted for a private burial, so I didn't even know where he was. I just knew he was down there somewhere. Rotting.

Every time I thought about it, I gasped for breath.

"What is it?" Noelle Lange asked me.

We were standing next to the huge marble fireplace in one of four massive living rooms in the Pearsons' co-op on the Upper East Side of Manhattan. A few kids from school were staring at me, just as they had been ever since Thomas had first gone missing. It was like they were just salivating for the nervous breakdown they were sure I was going to have. But so far I hadn't even cried in their presence. I wouldn't give them the satisfaction. I waited for the soul-gripping fear to pass before answering.

"Nothing," I told her. "That just keeps happening."

"You're still in shock," Ariana Osgood whispered, her voice soothing. "It's perfectly normal."

Noelle nodded and put her hand on my back. Noelle. Being comforting. That was a new one. Mostly she just opted for sarcastic and mocking. She also looked softer than usual today. Less threatening. Her light-gray cashmere crewneck and simple black skirt were perfect, of course, but her brown hair was product-free and fell around her face, framing it in a way that made her appear gentler. She had also forgone the mascara and subtle eyeliner she always wore. Without it, she almost looked her real age. Like she was my equal.

I looked around the spacious room, feeling numb now and

extremely hot. Hundreds of people had turned out for the wake. They mingled in the muted opulence in their designer suits and black dresses, sipping wine and talking in low tones. Peppered among the gray-haired gentlemen and Botoxed ladies were dozens of kids from school, all of whom looked shocked and shaken. Like Noelle, some of Easton's most renowned Shiseido worshippers hadn't even bothered with makeup. They perched on sofas and settees, dabbing at their eyes with handkerchiefs, consoling one another. The guys, meanwhile, stood around with their hands in their pockets, looking skittish. As if their confidence had been somehow shaken. Maybe if Thomas Pearson was capable of dying, they weren't quite as invincible as they had once thought. Reality had just set in for these guys who normally walked around in a dream world, a world where they were completely untouchable.

"Could this be any more morbid?" Kiran Hayes said, swinging her wineglass around a bit too brazenly. "This many people didn't turn up when the pope died. It's like everyone has some sicko fascination just because he was a kid."

Kiran tipped her wineglass toward her mouth and downed what was left in one gulp. An actual billboard model, she was the most beautiful person I had ever met in real life. And after knowing her for a month, I was starting to feel like she might also be the one most likely to end up in rehab. A few pieces of her dark hair had fallen out of her carefully twisted bun, and her green eyes were unfocused. Still, every guy in the room was checking her out when they thought no one was watching.

"I bet one of these blond chignons walking around here is covering it for the rags," Noelle said stoically. "A good prep school scandal is their wet dream."

There was the Noelle I knew and feared.

"Noelle!" Ariana scolded, her blue eyes piercing. Her own blond hair was also back in a loose chignon. In her dark clothing, with her diamond earrings securely fastened in her ears, Ariana looked less wispy and more in charge than she ever had before.

"What? No one heard me," Noelle said, smoothing her long, dark hair behind one shoulder. "And I'll bet you my entire trust fund I'm right. Just wait. 'The Thomas Pearson Tragedy' will have a four-page spread in *Hamptons Magazine* next month."

"I can't believe anyone would want to exploit his death," I said. "It's not like he's famous or something."

"He was around here," Noelle said with a sigh.

At that moment, Taylor Bell, who had been sniffling and quietly weeping all day, burst into another round of tears. Her dark-blond curls shook as she buried her cherubic face in a handkerchief. Ariana reached out and rubbed Taylor's arms.

Taylor's display of emotion made me so uncomfortable I had to look away. She and the rest of these girls hadn't even liked Thomas. They had, in fact, hated him. Warned me to stay away from him. And now, like everyone else, they were all completely shattered. As if Thomas had meant the world to them.

Still, it wasn't like I should have been that surprised. Love him or hate him, Thomas had been a classmate. One of them. They had known him for years. So of course they would be shocked and freaked. I was just surprised at *how* freaked.

My strained eyes fell on Missy Thurber—big nostrils, bigger attitude—leaning back against the tastefully papered wall in her chic black suit, her nose all red from crying. At her side, as always, was Lorna Gross, whispering in her ear, looking very somber. I suddenly wanted to hurl something at them from across the room. Where the hell did they get off pretending to mourn? Neither of them had ever spoken to Thomas in their lives.

Between them and Taylor and Kiran's continued rantings, I was beginning to feel a bit claustrophobic. Then I saw Constance Talbot, my former roommate, making her way across the room toward me. The last time I had seen Constance she had told me off with tears in her eyes for dating the guy of her dreams, Walt Whittaker. Walt Whittaker, who was here somewhere, chatting up a few members of the older generation, as usual. Whit and I were definitely no longer an item (not that we'd ever really been one), but I had no idea whether or not Constance knew this or not.

I stood up straight as she stepped up to me, my whole body tense. Constance met my gaze, then threw her arms around me.

"Reed! I am so, so, so, *so* sorry!" she said over my shoulder.

I was so surprised, it took me a moment to respond. But then I hugged her back. Hard. In a million years I never would have been able to predict the relief that rushed through me at her gesture of friendship. Apparently Constance was a lot more important to me than I'd realized.

"Thanks," I said as she pulled away.

Her green eyes were bright and red-rimmed, her wavy, dark-red hair held back in a simple ponytail. It was hard to tell if she was paler than usual or if it was the lighting, but somehow the freckles on her nose stood out more today, making her look almost precious.

"Are you okay?" she asked me, biting her lip.

"Yeah, I guess. I don't know," I said. A bubbly sob rose up into my throat and I swallowed it back. "It's all just a little surreal."

Surreal didn't even begin to describe it, but it was the only word I could come up with. Every other second I experienced a new and intense emotion. Just forty-eight hours ago I had been on a train back to Easton from the city, telling Josh—Thomas's roommate—that I was over Thomas. That I was moving on. And I had felt really good about that decision. Thomas, after all, had disappeared from school without warning. Without a goodbye. I had found that note from him days later, but it had raised more questions than it had answered. And for weeks he hadn't bothered to get in touch with me, even to let me know that he was all right. I had decided that a guy like that was not worth my time. That I deserved better.

But now I had found out that the reason Thomas had been incommunicado was that he was *dead.* And every time I thought about how indignant and angry and self-righteous I'd been over the past few weeks, I felt this soul-sucking guilt unlike anything I had ever felt before.

"It must make it harder, not knowing how he died," Constance said. She turned around to stand next to me and survey the room.

"You bet your ass it is," Kiran said, a bit too loudly. She grabbed another wineglass from a passing waiter and drained half of it.

"Kiran, keep your voice down," Ariana said.

"What? I'm just saying I'd like to know, you know, exactly *how* they think it happened, that's all," Kiran ranted. "Wouldn't it make you feel better to just know, once and for all, what they're thinking? If they have any theories?"

"You're rambling," Ariana said, taking the glass right out of Kiran's hands and placing it on the mantel, out of reach. Kiran looked after it longingly.

"I wonder if his parents know," Noelle said, narrowing her eyes as the golden-haired Mrs. Pearson strode into the room to whisper in the ear of the caterer. "They'd have to tell the parents, right?"

No one spoke. It wasn't as if we knew the inner workings of the justice system.

"Look at them," Kiran said, lifting her chin toward Mrs. Pearson, who had now been joined by her silver-haired husband. She snapped at a waiter and procured a fresh glass of wine. Ariana rolled her eyes. "They're just chatting like this is some charity function. When I go, I hope my parents don't look that poised."

"Kiran! Oh my God!" Taylor said, her quivering jaw dropping.

"What? I'm just saying," Kiran replied, rolling her eyes.

"Talk about morbid," Noelle said.

I watched as Mrs. Pearson chuckled and laid her hand gently on the arm of one of their friends. Mr. Pearson checked his watch and glanced around as if looking to see if there was anyone more interesting to talk to. Suddenly, my heart started to flutter in this insane way. A way that made my breath catch and my skin sear.

They had lost their only son and they didn't even care.

I looked away and my eyes fell on a tall, broad guy, about my age, who was leaning against the wall alone, staring at me. I looked away quickly, thinking maybe we'd just happened to glance at each other at the exact same moment, but when I looked back, he was still staring. He had a thin face, chalk-white skin, and blue eyes rimmed in red. His black hair was slicked back and he wore a black suit. Add some dark lighting and eerie music and he could have been a vampire lying in wait. I waited for him to look away. And waited. Still he stared.

"Who is that?" I asked Noelle finally.

"That? That's Blake."

"Blake who? Why is he staring at me?" I asked, nervous.

"Blake *Pearson*," Noelle said. "Thomas's brother?"

The entire building might as well have collapsed beneath my feet. I leaned against the wall, feeling for a moment that I might black out. I wasn't sure my body could take another shock.

"Thomas's *what*?"

"He never told you he had an older brother?" Noelle asked. "God, that boy was really down with the secrets."

"Why would Thomas talk about Blake?" Ariana reached up and scratched the back of her neck. "They hated each other."

"They did?" I asked, half out of it. I wanted to know more, but my brain was too frazzled to formulate words. Had he talked to Thomas before he died? What did he know? But when I managed to look up again, Blake was gone. A chill raced down my back.

"'Member that huge brawl they had freshman year?" Kiran drawled. "I really thought they were going to kill each other."

Ariana shot her a silencing glare. Not at all an appropriate comment.

"What happened?" I asked.

"Blake was having an affair with the dean's secretary, and Thomas threatened to tell their parents. Classic 'I wanna be the favorite son' threat," Noelle said.

"Wait a minute, wait a minute," I said. "Thomas's brother had an affair with Ms. Lewis-Hanneman? But she's . . . old."

"Yeah, but look at the woman. She's totally hot. And it's not like she's *ancient*. She was still in her twenties a couple years ago," Kiran said. "Deteriorating, sure, but not quite ready for the junkyard."

"I think we should change the subject now, ladies," Ariana said, noticing that some of the older attendees were beginning to stare.

This was totally insane. Thomas had a brother. An older brother who supposedly couldn't stand him. Why had Blake been staring at me? Did he know who I was? Had Thomas told him about me? I thought I had known Thomas so well and all along he'd had a brother I had never even heard about. Yet another mystery that would never be explained.

"I have to get out of here," I said, pushing myself away from the wall.

I walked right through the crowd and over to the far side of the room where Josh stood chatting with some other guys from school. His curly blond hair had been tamed with some kind of gel and he looked even taller and slightly broader than usual in his blue suit. While the rest of us had been whisked to the city in a limousine commissioned by Dash McCafferty's parents, Josh had driven his own Range Rover down—the one he kept in a garage off campus in case of emergency. He had been prescient enough to realize that either he or someone he cared about might want to bail from this charade early. Boy had a gift.

"Hey," I said, touching his arm.

He took one look at me and his blue eyes widened. "You okay?"

Just being near him made me feel slightly better. Solid, comforting, levelheaded Josh. He would take care of everything.

"Fine," I said flatly. "I just need to go. Can we go?"

"Yeah. Definitely. Let's go," he said.

He placed his water glass on a table nearby, said a few words to the guys, and placed his hand against the small of my back as we turned. He walked me back to my friends near the fireplace, all of whom were already gathering their purses.

"You guys wanna bail?" he asked.

"My hero," Noelle said wryly.

"In *your* car?" Taylor asked, her eyes still wet.

"Yes, in *his* car. What do you think, he's gonna hijack a helicopter?" Noelle snapped.

Taylor looked at Kiran, who rolled her eyes and finished the wine she'd grabbed back from the mantel. "Just what I need," she muttered.

What the hell was wrong with these girls? Were they really that put out by the fact that they'd have to spend a couple of hours in a car that wasn't a limo? Five minutes living my life at home and they'd probably all break out in hives.

"Where are Dash and Gage?" Josh asked.

"Who cares?" Noelle said, abandoning Dash, who was her boyfriend, with two words. "They're big boys. They'll live without us. Let's just get the hell out of here."

"Constance?" I said, turning to her. "Wanna come?"

Constance looked warily at the four girls surrounding me—the four most powerful girls in all of Easton. Apparently the idea was too intimidating for her to handle.

"Actually, I'm supposed to have dinner with my parents and the Whittakers tonight," she said finally. "They're bringing me back."

"Really?"

Under any other circumstances, this news would have made me smile. Constance blushed. "It was our parents' idea."

Later, when I had the energy and the motivation, I would have to grill her about this. But for now, she was off the hook. The good news was that I could tell that all the Whittaker-related tension between us was gone for good.

"Okay. I'll see you back there," I told her.

Then I did something I hade never done before. I voluntarily hugged a person.

Suddenly, I couldn't wait to get out of this place. I could practically taste freedom. On our way out, Ariana veered off course, away from the door.

"Where are we going?" I asked.

"Reed, we have to pay our respects," she said over her shoulder. "We're not heathens."

Great. Exactly what I wanted to do. As we approached the family, Mrs. Pearson chatted with a horse-faced woman with capped teeth and a widow's peak.

"Well, yes, of course. This is the only time of year to be in Paris. Any other season it's just *overrun* with tourists," Mrs. Pearson was saying.

"Trina hasn't considered herself a tourist in any part of Europe since the day she bought her first couture," Thomas's father added, sharing a chuckle with his friend.

"We'd be there now, if it wasn't for this," Thomas's mother said, gesturing blithely at the room.

My heart was in a vise. There was no way. There was no way these people were standing there joking about their travel habits and dismissing Thomas's wake as an inconvenience. Suddenly, I couldn't breathe.

"Screw them. Just get it over with," Noelle said in my ear as Ariana politely shook the Hands of Evil.

When I stepped before the Pearsons, I must have been red with rage. Still, part of me expected them to recognize me as the person who had been with them when we had first realized that Thomas was missing. The person who had meant enough to their son that he had invited me to brunch with them. But when his mother's cold, hard eyes fell on me there was no spark of anything. Except, perhaps, mild displeasure. Apparently my simple black dress and unhighlighted brown hair didn't meet her exacting standards. These were the things that were on her mind today of all days. Well, these things and Paris.

"I'm sorry for your loss," I told her through my teeth.

Then I somehow refrained from grinding my heel into her toe on my way out the door.

TIME BOMBS

Josh adjusted his seat and checked the mirror for the tenth time. Behind us, the line of cars waiting to get out of the Eighty-first Street garage started to grow.

"Any day now, Hollis," Noelle said through a sigh. She leaned her arm on the front windowsill. Of course she had taken the front, no questions asked.

"Sorry. When I picked up the car back at Easton the seat was all pushed forward for some reason, and I still haven't gotten it back where I like it," he said.

Kiran glanced around at everyone as if this news made her feel unsafe somehow. Ariana caught her eye for a long moment and then Kiran relaxed again. That penetrating stare of Ariana's had multiple purposes.

"Great. So you're too cheap to spring for memory seats and we're the ones who have to suffer," Noelle griped.

"Back off, Noelle," Josh said through his teeth. "I wanna get out of here as much as you do."

My fingers curled into tense fists and I tried to breathe. All I got was a lungful of noxious fumes. I just wanted to go, to put this all behind me. My leg started to bounce up and down. Sitting still was not an option. When I was sitting, it felt like something was gnawing on my heart.

My heart pounded harder and harder. *Breathe, breathe, breathe.*

"There's no air in here," Ariana stated.

Amen, sister.

"It's the long pedal on the right, Hollis," Noelle said.

"Do you always have to be such a bitch, Noelle?" Josh snapped.

Whoa. That was uncharacteristic.

"Do you always have to be such a Boy Scout, Josh?" she snapped back.

Breathe, breathe, breathe.

A horn honked from one of the cars behind us, echoing throughout the garage.

"Josh?" I half-whined, at the end of my rope.

"Fine! Fine, we're going," Josh said. "Remind me never to get in a car with five women again."

As he eased out onto the street, Josh caught my eye in the rearview mirror. I could tell he was wondering if I was okay. Already I was breathing easier, so I attempted to smile reassuringly. Unfortunately, somewhere between the elevator and the parking garage I had finally let a few tears loose and now they were drying on the skin under my eyes, making it feel tight and itchy, which made it hard to smile.

"What the hell am I sitting on?" Kiran yanked a dirty white batting glove out from under her perfect little butt. She groaned and threw it over her shoulder, where it narrowly missed the side of Taylor's face. It fell over the second row of seats into the back, where it joined the rest of Josh's baseball equipment. "God, do you *ever* clean out your car?"

Josh ignored her comment and Ariana sighed. Finally, we all fell into an exhausted silence. As Josh whisked us northward I stared out the window at Yankee Stadium on the other side of the East River and tried to silently name every professional baseball team I could think of. Anything to keep from actually thinking.

Thinking that I was never going to see Thomas again. For the rest of my life. We had spoken our last words to each other. Had our last kiss. God, I wished I had known that then.

"Well, at least *that's* over," Kiran said finally, hugging herself rather tightly, as if she was trying not to touch anything she didn't have to touch. I could smell her breath from three feet away.

"It's not over," Josh said flatly. "Thomas is still dead."

I tried to ignore the squeezing in my heart. Ariana stared at the back of Josh's head as if he'd just said something totally inappropriate. He did, however, have a point. This misery would never be over. Thomas was dead. Forever.

"I wish the police would tell us what the hell is going on," Noelle said, staring out the window. "I bet they don't know a thing."

"Wouldn't be the first time the cops effed things up," Josh put in.

Noelle turned to Josh suddenly, as if a thought had just occurred to her. "Do you think one of his drug buddies had something to do with this?"

No one moved. I saw Josh's grip on the steering wheel tighten. Noelle had just voiced a suspicion that had been lurking in the back of my mind ever since I'd heard that Thomas was dead. For days I had been forcing myself not to think about it. Because whenever I did, my imagination conjured horrible things. Things that made my stomach clench and caused serious sweat issues. Hundreds of gruesome grudge murders and torture scenes I had seen in the movies or on those endless stupid cop dramas—they all came flooding back. And I couldn't handle the idea that Thomas might have died in some twisted, excruciating way at the hands of some red-eyed druggie psycho.

But all Noelle was doing was pointing out the obvious. Thomas *had* been dealing drugs. And when a drug dealer turns up dead, there are logical conclusions that can be easily drawn.

"I'd say it's a definite possibility," Ariana said coolly.

Josh glanced in the side mirror, flipped his blinker on, and changed lanes. He cleared his throat.

"You know, no one has said that Thomas was mur—that his death was, you know . . ."

I met Kiran's eye and knew she was thinking the same thing I was. There was just something so horrifying about the word *murder* that no one wanted to say it.

Noelle exhaled loudly. "Come on, Hollis. Like he what, died of natural causes? A perfectly healthy seventeen-year-old guy? I mean, I know you of all people don't want to open that particular can of worms, but come on."

Josh turned his head fully to glare at her. She didn't deign to look back.

"Watch the road, Hollis. Unless you want to get us *all* killed," she said.

With a clenched jaw, Josh turned his attention back to his driving. No one said a word for a good two minutes, during which time I wondered what the hell that little exchange was about.

"Healthy, Noelle? Really?" Kiran said. "Thomas Pearson wasn't exactly the poster boy for holistic living. He had more chemicals in his system that night than Kate Moss on a New Year's Eve bender."

"How do you know what he had in his system?" Josh asked.

Kiran pulled her hair in front of her face and inspected it. "Just an informed assumption, Hollis. When did he ever *not* have crap in his system?"

Look who's talking, Kiran.

My heart clenched in anger. Hadn't anyone in this car ever heard of not speaking ill of the dead?

"And even if he *was* healthy, it happens all the time," Taylor piped up, sitting forward and resting her hands on the back of the front seat. A mangled tissue was crushed in her fist. "Kids our age have aneurysms . . . even strokes!"

Her hope was so incongruent I had to stifle a rueful laugh. Happily suggesting strokes. This was what we had come to.

"Well, if it wasn't some freak of nature, then I bet it was that shady townie character he was always hooking up with," Noelle said blithely.

What shady townie character? I knew of no shady townie character.

"These people are like walking time bombs," Noelle continued. "Living up in the sticks with nothing to do, no outlet for all their little psychotic tendencies. And you know they resent the shit out of us."

"Maybe one of them snapped," Ariana suggested, lifting a shoulder.

"I'm just saying it's possible," Noelle added, looking at Ariana in the rearview mirror.

I took a deep breath. Images were starting to flood my mind. Blood. Rope. Knives. Guns. Gags. Images I would rather not have dwelled on.

"Do you think the police know that Thomas was dealing?" Noelle asked Josh.

He cleared his throat again. There was no doubt he wanted out of this conversation. "Probably not. If there was one thing Thomas knew how to do, it was cover his tracks."

"Well, somebody should tell them," Noelle said, her tone as casual as if she were suggesting an ice cream stop on the way home.

"You want us to tell on Thomas?" I said without thinking.

"Aw! That's so cute! What are you, five?" Noelle said. "Come on, Reed. What does he care? It's not like they can arrest him."

Everyone fell silent. Noelle was getting just a touch too morbid for me.

"I'm serious!" Noelle said. "If that freak show did have something to do with it, he should be brought in and questioned. Unless you want him to get away with it."

I glanced at Josh, who stared back at me in the mirror. How could we tell the world that Thomas was dealing? He was gone. Didn't he deserve to rest in peace? To have his perfect prep school boy image untarnished?

"His parents would freak," Josh said. "I don't think I could do that to them."

"You don't owe those ice sculptures anything," Noelle said.

Josh's face went flat—in a way that made me think that maybe he did owe the Pearsons something. Interesting. What could that possibly mean?

"The guy did die," Kiran said, her eyes half-closed and bleary. "Somebody should probably pay for it."

Taylor let out a choked sob, then dropped back in her seat and started crying all over again.

"Are you okay?" I asked her.

Actually, it kind of snapped out of me. But Taylor didn't seem to notice. She simply nodded and grabbed a new tissue from the box at her feet.

"It's just so sad," she said. "I just wish none of this had happened. I just—"

And then she went incoherent all over again.

After that we all lapsed into silence, watching the world go by as Taylor's sobs slowly quieted to nothing.

FAT PHOEBE

When I walked into my room at Billings, the sun was just starting to set. I was surprised to feel relief as I closed the door behind me. Apparently, this room, with its huge bay window, hardwood floors, and the scent of Natasha's lavender perfume, had actually become a comfort zone.

Two seconds later, the door opened and my roommate, Natasha Crenshaw, walked in with her cell folded in her hand. Her phone never worked inside our room, so she was constantly going outside or up to the Billings House roof to make calls.

"Hey."

It was amazing how much tentative sympathy one syllable could convey. She stepped around me to take a survey of my face, probably to check if I was in the midst of a breakdown. Her dark skin was clean and makeup-free, and she wore a pair of yoga pants topped by a baggy sweatshirt.

"Hey," I replied, dumping my stuff on my bed.

"How was it?" she asked.

I blew out a sigh and dropped down on the edge of my mattress. My feet cried out in gratitude when I kicked off the heels I'd borrowed from Kiran's Closet of Dreams. Girl had more shoes than I had pores, but it seemed like every pair was more torturous than the last.

"It was . . . you know . . . terrible," I told her.

"I'm sorry I couldn't come," Natasha said. She moved to her own bed so that we were sitting directly across from each other on either side of the wide room. "I just can't do funerals anymore."

"Anymore?" I asked.

Natasha took a deep breath. "I lost someone close to me a couple years ago," she said cagily. "Ever since then I've pretty much avoided all the 'Yea though I walk' stuff."

Although my curiosity was piqued, I knew she would have given me more details if she wanted to. And if there was one thing I wanted to respect right then, it was other people's delicate feelings.

"So, if you want to talk ever," Natasha said tentatively. "I mean, I know we haven't had the greatest track record. . . ."

We both laughed quickly at that one. Not the greatest track record—if that was what she wanted to call blackmailing me into snooping around my friends' dorm rooms. Of course, the offense was fairly forgivable, since she had been blackmailed into blackmailing me. Such was the life of a Billings Girl.

Still, the whole mess had resulted in me learning a lot about who Natasha was—an out-of-the-closet lesbian with a still-closeted girlfriend whom she'd do pretty much anything to protect—and she had learned a lot about me. Like the fact that I could keep a secret. And the fact that I was loyal to my friends. Somewhere along the line, I had begun to trust her. With a certain amount of caution.

"But, I mean, how are you?" she asked.

I groaned and dropped back on my pillows, one leg dangling off the side of the bed as I gazed at the ceiling. "Got about a year?"

"Sure," Natasha said.

Huh. Maybe she really did want to listen. *Stupefied* was the word that came to mind.

"Um . . . okay." I lifted a hand to tick off my various emotions. "I feel . . . crushingly sad that I never got to say goodbye, angry that he left, guilty for the anger, angry some more at his parents, angry some *more* at all the hypocritical assholes around here, and then just tired and devastated and really, really scared that I'm never gonna stop feeling like this. Does that cover it?" I asked, turning my head so I could see her.

Natasha frowned and nodded. "Sounds about right."

"Oh, wait!" I said, sitting up again. I pressed my hands into the bedspread. I could feel that my hair was staticking out, but I didn't care. "There's also the second wave of guilt. You know, the guilt over the fact that I had decided Thomas wasn't worth my time when I hadn't heard from him, when *now* it turns out that I hadn't heard from him because he was—"

My throat closed.

"Because he was—"

Oh, crap. The tears started flowing.

Natasha got up and sat down next to me.

"It's okay," she said.

"No, it's not." And suddenly I was bawling. The hot tears just came and came and came. I tried to hold them back. Choked and gasped and tried to swallow, but I couldn't. "I can't believe this is happening. This shouldn't be happening."

Natasha put her arm around me and rubbed my shoulder. I just cried. I felt like an idiot, but there was nothing I could do about it. There was no stopping me now. All I could see was Thomas's face. His hands. His arm around me. His smile. I couldn't believe I was never going to see him again. Could. Not. Believe. It. I choked for air and my throat burned. There were sounds coming out of me that I had never heard before.

I just wanted to expel it all, all the anger at the Pearsons and at myself and at Thomas—even at Missy Thurber. I wanted to get it all out of my system. All I wanted was to stop feeling so wretched.

Finally, after who knew how long, I started to quiet down. I lifted my head and sniffled and wiped below my eyes with my fingertips.

"Better?" Natasha asked.

My breath was shaky. "Yeah. Thanks."

I got up, grabbed a tissue from my desk, and blew into it. Hard. I sucked in a few broken breaths and blew again. "Did you know that Thomas had a brother?" I asked her.

"Yeah. Blake. He graduated last year," Natasha said. "Why? Didn't you?"

I sniffled. Toyed with the soaked tissue. "He never told me."

"Wow. Maybe everyone has someone in their lives they can't talk about," Natasha said.

She was referencing Leanne Shore, her girlfriend, but I instantly thought of my mother. My mother, who was probably passed out in her bed drooling right now, even though it was four o'clock in the afternoon. An open bottle of pills would be on her nightstand and some bad Court TV reality show would be playing in the background. I wondered if my father had even told her what had happened. That had been a fun phone call. It had taken me twenty minutes to convince him not to pull me out of school. When he'd finally agreed I had felt relief beyond anything I'd felt before. I did not want to go back to my dung-colored life in Croton, Pennsylvania. Even if there was, potentially, a murderer running around campus. Easton with a murderer was far better than Croton High without one. It was an indisputable fact.

"Was Blake there? Did you talk to him?" Natasha asked.

At that moment, the door was flung open, and Noelle and Ariana burst in, followed by Rose Sakowitz and the Twin Cities—London Simmons and Vienna Clark. They had all changed out of their funeral drab and into much more colorful outfits. In their arms they carried a half-dozen bakery boxes and various bottles of champagne.

"Reed Brennan! Welcome to your first Fat Phoebe party!"

London squealed, holding up two bottles of champagne. Her ever-pushed-up breasts nearly spilled out of her tank top, and her dark hair was done in two low ponytails. One look at her in that getup and half the guys I knew would have orgasmed on the spot.

"You guys—" Natasha said, rolling her eyes.

"Come on! It's the perfect remedy for *whatever* ails you," Vienna said, opening one of the boxes. Inside were at least a dozen perfect-looking chocolate éclairs.

"What's a Fat Phoebe party?" I asked.

I noticed that Kiran and Taylor were suspiciously absent, but upon arrival at the Easton gates each had been catatonic for different reasons. Hopefully, they were both already sleeping it off.

"It's an age-old tradition with a highly inappropriate title," Ariana explained.

"It all started, like, ten years ago when this manic-depressive girl got into Billings," Vienna explained.

"Phoebe Appleby," Rose put in.

"Unfortunate name," Noelle said with a shudder.

"Really slipped through the cracks, that one," London said.

"Anyway, whenever Phoebe got depressed—"

"Which, according to legend, was every day—"

"She ordered up a bunch of pastries from the local patisserie and broke out a bottle of Cristal—"

"And threw a Fat Phoebe party! Whooo!" London cried, lifting the bottles again.

"Though I don't think that's what *she* called it," Ariana put in.

"Basically, it's champagne and chocolate," Noelle explained. She walked over and hooked her arm around my neck. "Obscene amounts of both."

"It'll take your mind off more unpleasant things," Ariana added, wrinkling her nose in a dainty way.

More unpleasant things. Like we were talking about a particularly nasty foot fungus or something.

"Let's do this!" Rose cheered. "I need a chocolate fix, stat."

Everyone cheered.

My skin crawled and I ducked away from Noelle. I felt like screaming. What was wrong with these people? They really thought a sugar high and a buzz were going to make it all better?

"Sorry, you guys. I'm not up for a party," I said.

"What? Why?" London asked, pouting as she lowered her bottles.

Take pity on her. She's a ditz. She doesn't know how idiotic she looks.

"Because I . . . I'm tired," I told them. "Exhausted, actually. I think I'm just gonna go to bed."

Noelle gave me a reproachful stare. She wasn't used to hearing the word *no*.

"Reed—"

"You guys have fun," I said flatly, moving forward, crowding them toward the door.

Rose, London, and Vienna took the hint, jostling their way out. Ariana paused and looked at me with her clear blue eyes.

"You really should try to get your mind off things," she said. "You'll feel better."

"I already do," I said honestly.

Not 100 percent. But after venting my emotions and blubbering all over Natasha, I *was* much improved. For now. But if I thought for one second longer about the idea of partying, the anger was going to come back full force.

"You're sure?" Noelle said. "You really don't want to come?"

"I'm sure." I placed my hand on the door. "Please, Noelle. Just go."

Ariana and Noelle locked eyes. Never a good sign. I knew I had stepped over a line in their eyes, and for a split second I was reminded of how scared I'd been of them just a couple of weeks ago. Thomas's death had cured me of that, at least temporarily. At that very moment, I couldn't imagine remotely caring what they might do or say to me.

"Get some sleep," Noelle said finally. "We'll see you later."

And with that, she closed the door. Nothing more. Maybe Thomas's death had cured them too.

DECISION

Cheerios expand when left to soak in milk for too long. If you gaze blankly at them long enough, you can watch it happen. Also, the curious stares of your peers become less noticeable when you're working on approximately forty-five minutes of sleep in three days. And the cafeteria manager doesn't like it when he finds someone sitting on the cold brick outside the door waiting for him to unlock it.

Ninety percent out of it and I was still learning things.

A few uneventful days had passed since Thomas's funeral, and I had still hardly eaten or slept. That is, uneventful aside from the fact that several kids had been taken out of school by their parents. Mostly freshmen. Skittish newbie parents, according to Noelle. "As if this school has never survived a scandal before," she'd said yesterday, as we watched a scarecrow-haired Asian guy being loaded into a Hummer. None of my friends had been spirited away, but it was almost eerie to see the sedans and limos idling in the circle in front of the dorms, the students being escorted with their bags while their parents looked around suspiciously, as if some masked killer was suddenly going to come shrieking out of the shadows. No one had officially said that Thomas's death had been suspicious in nature, but it was clear that was what people wanted to assume. My heart tightened and released as I thought of him. This was all it ever did anymore. I wondered if it was going to affect my long-term health.

A couple of girls whispered and shot me looks as they walked by, so I turned my head so that my hair would hide my face. The area under my eyes felt full and tight and heavy at all times, like I might either pass out or burst into tears at any second.

The door to the cafeteria opened and I looked up instinctively, an image of Thomas flashing through my mind's eye. A queasy warmth hit me and I felt so wretchedly stupid I wanted to scream. It wasn't Thomas. It was never going to *be* Thomas. *Figure it out, Reed.*

"Are you all right?"

Somehow I lifted my eighty-pound head and looked up at Josh. He hovered at the end of the otherwise deserted cafeteria table with a tray full of doughnuts and chocolate milk. Boy took in more sugar before 9 a.m. than most five-year-olds did in a day. You'd think a place as pricey as Easton would make sure all their charges got four squares, but apparently that was not one of the perks the elite were paying for.

"M'fine," I mumbled. "Just wishing this bowl was a pillow."

I pushed my tray aside and rested my elbows on the table, taking a long, deep breath to try to crowd out the nausea. Josh sat down across from me and lifted his messenger bag over his head, placing it on the floor. He wore a blue and yellow rugby shirt with a green paint stain on one of the yellow stripes. His curls were product-free today, which meant they stuck out adorably in all directions.

Adorably. I wanted to flog myself. Thomas was dead. I was not supposed to be noticing that other guys were adorable.

Under the table, Josh fumbled with his bag. He slapped his hand to his mouth, then took a chug of his chocolate milk to help him swallow.

"What was that?" I asked.

"Vitamins," Josh said. "One a day keeps the doctor away."

"You are a parent's wet dream," I told him.

"Tell that to my parents," he deadpanned.

I smiled. It was nice that he could make me smile even in my current state of semi-consciousness.

Josh lowered his body toward the table a bit, in confab mode. I leaned in as well. "So, I've thought about it, and I've decided to go to the cops like Noelle said," he whispered.

He bit into a powdered-sugar doughnut and powdered sugar sprayed everywhere. I looked at him and wondered if I was dreaming. Did he really just tell me that he was going to rat out Thomas and then take a big old bite of doughnut? I couldn't even swallow one spoonful of cereal this morning and he seemed, well, fine. In fact, for the past few days, Josh had been keeping it together better than anyone else I knew, which made little to no sense. Thomas had been his roommate. His friend. And I hadn't even seen him cry once. But what did I know? Maybe he went back to his room and blubbered in private all night long. It wouldn't have been the first time someone around Easton kept a secret. I was starting to wonder if secrets were a prerequisite for admittance.

"You really think that's necessary?" I asked.

"Noelle was right," Josh said, chewing. "That guy she was talking about? Rick? He was Thomas's local supplier and he's a total wackjob. I would bet money he had something to do with this."

I took a deep breath, straightened my back for a second, then slumped again. "I don't know, Josh. Do we really want Thomas's parents to know all this stuff? I know he was into some scary crap, but he was trying to change. Did he tell you he was on his way to rehab the night he left?"

Josh blurted a laugh and took a sip of milk, smiling in mirth. I felt very hot all over.

"What?" I said.

Josh blinked at me and then his face fell. "Oh. You're serious," he said.

"Yes, I'm serious," I said, beyond offended.

Josh put his milk down and wiped his hands on his jeans. "Reed, I hate to be the one to tell you this, but Thomas was the last person who was *ever* going to rehab. He was so wasted the last night he was here you could have wrung him out and served shots."

The cafeteria had just become a Gravitron, whirling and tilting and heading for the sky. There was no way to focus, so I closed my eyes.

"What?" I said, my mouth dry.

"I came back from the library and he was on the phone screaming at Rick, so gone he couldn't even stand up straight," Josh whispered. "That's why I think Noelle might be right. Thomas was pretty livid, and I bet he said some stuff he wouldn't have said if he wasn't such a mess. I didn't think much of it at the time, because those two were always at each other's throats over something, but maybe this time he really pissed Rick off somehow."

I pressed the heel of my hand into my forehead, trying to make sense of all of this. Thomas was *drunk?* But he had been so sincere about quitting. And he'd left me that note. He was going to some holistic treatment center. He was getting help.

Had that all been a lie?

"This doesn't make any sense," I said aloud.

"What?" Josh asked.

Wait a minute, wait a minute. Why would he have left me that note if he wasn't actually planning on leaving? I would have been *kind of* suspicious if I had found the note that night and then seen him on campus the next day. So he must have been planning on going somewhere. But where?

"Maybe it was just a last hurrah," I suggested. "Maybe he wanted to get drunk one last time before going to rehab?"

It sounded totally pathetic even as I said it. So pathetic that Josh actually had pity in his eyes.

"Reed, what makes you so sure that Thomas was going to rehab?" he asked gently.

The double doors opened and sunlight poured in. Noelle, Ariana, Taylor, and Kiran strode through and headed straight for the breakfast line. I didn't want them to hear any of this and start speculating. We had to talk fast.

"He left me a note," I confessed quickly. "I found it in one of my books. He said he was going to a treatment center and not to try to find him. He said he was leaving that night."

Josh stared at me for a long moment. Slowly, he shook his head. "Leave it to Pearson. I bet the last words out of his mouth were a lie."

A thump of dread warmed my insides. "What do you mean?"

Josh looked at me as if he'd just realized who he was talking to. "Nothing. Forget it," he said.

"Josh—"

"It's just . . ." He crumpled a napkin and squeezed it in his fist, just for the sake of crumpling and squeezing. "I just don't think that Thomas ever fully appreciated what he had when he had you, that's all."

Whoa. My mouth fell open slightly and I snapped it closed. Josh stared at me intently. No averted eyes, no quick change of subject. He really meant what he had just said. I was both flattered and completely thrown. He'd just implied that Thomas had lied to me nonstop . . . and complimented me in the same breath.

"Reed, you have to show that note to the police," Josh said.

"How do you know I haven't?" I asked.

"Have you?"

"No," I admitted miserably.

"It's evidence," Josh said. "It might be the last thing Thomas ever wrote. They need to see it."

My stomach felt acidic and warm. I had been dreading this moment for weeks, but Josh was right. When he put it that simply, it seemed obvious. Besides, I had only kept the note a secret to protect Thomas from his parents hunting him down. Now that was no longer an issue.

"You're right," I said, determined. "I'll go right after morning services."

Just thinking about it made me feel monumentally better. I was nervous to let the police know I had hidden something from them, but I couldn't wait to be free of it. Thomas had lied to me. Who knew how often or about what? It was no longer my responsibility to protect him. It was about time I got this whole thing over with, once and for all.

THE RIGHT THING TO DO

It wasn't until we were walking up the steps to Hell Hall that I realized what I was doing. The second I did, I tripped on the top stair and had to grab Josh's arm to prevent my knee from cracking on the slate.

"Careful!" Josh said, helping me up.

Our faces almost touched as I fought for balance. Our skin was so close that his body heat warmed my cheek. My heart was already pounding from nervousness. Now it pounded twice as fast. Josh looked at me and his grip on my arm tightened for a split second before he released me.

"I can't do this," I told him, stepping back. As if that might slow my pulse. I didn't need this. Not on top of everything else. What, exactly, was my capacity for confusing emotions? How much could I handle before a vital organ actually imploded?

"What do you mean?" Josh asked, his brow creasing. "I thought we decided—"

"I know what we decided," I said through my teeth. I could

smell the burning nylon as Thomas's note tried to sear its way out of my backpack.

Mr. Cross ascended the steps. He was the Ketlar House monitor and had been Thomas's advanced biology professor. Like all the other faculty members, he had an office in Hull Hall. ("Hell Hall" was the students' nickname for the ancient brick building in which most of the adults on campus spent the bulk of their time.) I pulled Josh aside, averting my gaze with a blush, to let the man pass. Still, my pulse raced at Josh's nearness.

I will not be attracted to Josh. I will not be attracted to Josh. Josh's dead roommate is my dead boyfriend. I will not go there.

Cross shot us a disapproving look under his clipped white eyebrows but kept moving. I didn't speak again until the heavy door had slammed behind him.

"But isn't this, like, withholding evidence?" I asked Josh under my breath. My earlier righteous bravado was gone, replaced, miraculously, by logic. "I could get in serious trouble here. I mean, before I was just protecting my boyfriend who was alive and rehabbing. Now it's like . . . what? Aiding and abetting or something?"

Obviously, I had spent too much time watching those bad cop shows. Damn you, Dick Wolf.

Josh stood up straight as this sank in. A cold breeze tousled his hair, and a thick gray cloud moved in front of the sun. I pulled my coat closer to me. Dozens of dry brown leaves chased one another across the stone path down below. Suddenly I really didn't want to be here. I turned to go.

"Wait. Reed, wait," Josh said, grabbing my arm lightly.

My foot hovered in the air over the next step and my stomach went weightless, like I was on a roller coaster that had just taken a dip.

"What?" I said over my shoulder.

"We have to show it to them. This is about finding out what happened to Thomas," Josh said earnestly. "It's about telling the truth. Finally."

I recalled a conversation Josh and I had with Walt Whittaker last week in the cafeteria. One in which Whit had accused Josh of being a hypocrite for not turning Thomas into the board of trustees for his illegal activities ages ago. Something in Josh's eyes told me that conversation had really affected him. Maybe even more so, now that Thomas was gone. Now that Noelle, too, had suggested it was the right thing to do.

The girl really did have power.

"Besides, what can they do to you?" Josh said. "You're a minor and you were just scared and confused and all that. It's not like they're gonna throw you in jail for keeping a love note or whatever."

His certainty somehow took the edge off my fear. "Fine," I said. I strode past him and opened the door before I could lose my newfound resolve. "But if I do end up behind bars, it's your job to get me out."

"Done and done," Josh said. Firmly. Like he really did intend to be my rescuer one day.

I walked ahead of him down the long, echoing hallway. Unbelievable. I was potentially walking to my doom, and definitely going to turn in my lying, deceased boyfriend . . . and then I did the most inappropriate, appalling thing possible.

I smiled.

DAYS

"Is that all you two have to say?" Dean Marcus asked, glaring at us from across his wide desk.

Isn't that enough?

The dean was definitely old, but since Thomas had gone missing, the police had invaded our campus, and parents had started yanking their kids and their tuition, he seemed to have aged ten years. His wrinkles were deeper, the gray at his temples had spread, and his brown eyes seemed to swim sourly in their sockets. The note from Thomas was laid out flat on his leather blotter, the only piece of paper on his otherwise impeccably organized desk. In the corner, the tall, imposing Chief Sheridan whispered intently with his shorter, kinder counterpart, Detective Hauer. After muttering a few expletives toward the beginning of our stories, they had been conferencing on and off throughout the rest of the meeting.

"We're very sorry we didn't come in sooner, sir," Josh said, sounding much more composed than I felt. "We just always hoped Thomas would be coming back—"

"And when he did, you were going to allow him to continue with his illegal activities," the dean said, his voice rising as the redness of his face deepened to near burgundy. "You were going to allow him to continue disgracing this institution."

I sank lower in my leather chair. I was going to get thrown out of Easton. I could feel it. I was never going to touch the ivy around the entrance to Billings again. Never find out if I could actually pass Mr. Barber's history class. Never sit with Noelle and Ariana and Kiran and Taylor and sip wine and eat expensive chocolates and laugh. Never see New York from windows high above Park Avenue again. What had I been thinking, coming here? How could I have forgotten how much there was to lose?

Croton, Pennsylvania, here I come! I wondered if that hand-written HELP WANTED sign was still hanging in the window of the Rite Aid.

"But that's not even the worst of it, Mr. Hollis," Dean Marcus continued, his indignation so strong he was starting to tremble. "If you had come to us with this information earlier we might have found Mr. Pearson *weeks* ago. You don't—"

My heart completely stopped beating.

"Dean," the chief said in a warning tone.

The dean went white under his age spots as he realized his slipup. He looked at the chief uncertainly.

Weeks ago? *Weeks?*

"Is that true?" I heard myself say, my voice sounding very meek. "Has Thomas been dead for that long?"

"I'm sorry, Miss Brennan, but we're not at liberty to divulge that information while our investigation continues," Chief Sheridan said firmly, stepping up to the desk.

Dean Marcus sat back in his chair, deflated. The chief's tone was reprimanding. Clearly, the dean had been relishing his position as man in charge of this meeting, and by speaking a few words too many he had just lost it. It seemed there was an authority higher than our school's number-one authority figure.

"But Dean Marcus is right. You should have told us these things during our first meetings," the chief continued, staring us down. "I know you thought you were protecting your friend, but by impeding our investigation you've done the exact opposite."

What little breakfast I'd managed to choke down was slowly rising up from my stomach. Was he right? Could I actually have prevented Thomas's death by coming forward? How could this be happening?

Tears came to my eyes, and I stared straight ahead at the green glass lamp on the dean's desk, watching it blur. I couldn't take this. I couldn't. I felt like my chest was filling up with something I couldn't define. Something that would surely drown me.

"You didn't know," Josh said, quietly.

I looked at him. He was staring right at me. Somehow, I felt calmer, and I willed him not to look away. If he looked away, I would sink.

"Excuse me, Mr. Hollis?" the chief snapped.

"I said she didn't know," Josh said a bit louder. "There was no way she could have known that Thomas was going to get hurt. As far as she knew, that was just a breakup note. How was she supposed to know?"

He glared at the chief. Glared at this man who could potentially end our lives as we knew them. Was he brave or just incredibly stupid? The moment he broke eye contact with me, tears slid silently down my cheeks.

Control yourself, Reed. You can do at least that. Don't let these people see you crumble. I wiped at my face, but the tears still came.

"Calm down, Mr. Hollis," Chief Sheridan said.

"I just don't see what you're accomplishing by making a girl cry. *Sir,*" Josh said.

"Josh. It's okay," I croaked.

He was going to get us expelled if he kept it up. Or arrested. Or both.

Chief Sheridan held Josh's gaze for a long moment, then turned his back to us and whispered to the dean. I strained to hear, but all I could pick up were a few stray words.

". . . punishment . . ."

". . . naive . . ."

". . . useful . . ."

Finally, the chief turned to us again. "You may go to class," he said, exhaling through his nose. The dean, meanwhile, turned his chair to the side, away from us. He looked like a deflated blowup toy version of himself.

Neither Josh nor I moved. It couldn't be that simple.

"I appreciate that you tried to do the right thing by coming in here today," the chief said. "It was a little late, but nevertheless, I see no point in charging you with anything. As minors you would get a slap on the wrist, and from the looks on your faces, I believe you've already gotten that."

Not just on the wrist. Across the face and in the stomach. With brass knuckles.

"But if you think of anything else—*anything at all*—you are to come to us immediately. Understood?" he asked, pressing one finger into the desktop.

"Yes, sir," Josh said, standing.

"Yes, sir," I echoed, my voice watery.

"Good," the chief said. "Now get out of here before I change my mind."

MY CALL

Weeks ago. Could have found him weeks ago. Thomas had been lying dead somewhere for at least a couple of weeks. But where? Where had they found him? The rumors were conflicting. I'd heard he was found in a field behind the public school. Near a stream in the hills. In some random abandoned building. And—the one that made me shudder the most—in the trunk of a beat-up old car.

Was I ever going to know the truth?

"Reed, you should really eat something," Ariana said in her mothering tone.

I blinked. The cafeteria was so hushed I had zoned out and forgotten where I was. My turkey sandwich on wheat toast stared up at me, untouched. Kiran and Natasha had just settled in across the table. I hadn't even heard them arrive.

"At least eat the bread," Ariana prodded gently.

"Eat the meat. You need the protein, not the carbs," Kiran said as she lifted a thick issue of *Vogue* out of her bag.

Natasha looked at me and smiled. Was Kiran ever *not* thinking about calorie counts? Ariana stared Kiran down while Kiran flipped past the pages and pages of ads at the front of her magazine as if she didn't notice.

"What? Carbs will just weigh her down. We're trying to get her energy up, right?" Kiran said finally, her green eyes wide. "Thus, protein."

No one could *ever* ignore a serious stare from Ariana. I flicked the bread off the top of my sandwich and ate a piece of turkey with my fingers. "Happy?"

Kiran wrinkled her dainty nose. "I would have preferred a fork, but that's fine."

Noelle walked over and sat in her usual chair across from Ariana at the end of the table. She let out a frustrated sigh and glared at Taylor as she slipped in behind me and dropped down in the next chair. Taylor's nose was red and her curls were matted and dark. As if they hadn't seen suds in days. She looked tired. Like someone who had spent the entire night staring at her alarm clock, calculating how many hours of sleep she could get if she just passed out *right now*.

Wait. That was me.

"What's up?" Kiran asked, looking from Taylor to Noelle.

"What's up is I'm sick of the morgue vibe already," Noelle said, flipping her long, dark hair over her shoulder. "Wallowing is good for nothing," she said pointedly, looking at me and Taylor. "Unless you *enjoy* getting your frown lines Botoxed."

"Noelle, they just buried Thomas last weekend," I said, the back of my throat tight.

"I know, okay? I was there," Noelle said. "But look at everyone. This is not healthy. If this keeps up, we're talking terminal downward spiral."

Just then the doors to the cafeteria slammed open and every single person in the room jumped. Dash McCafferty walked in, his blond hair flopping and eyes bright with what looked like excitement. Behind him were Josh and Gage Coolidge, who strolled along with a cocky expression on, as always, like he was working some invisible runway. Walt Whittaker brought up the rear, his cheeks ruddy from the cold, wearing a thick wool coat that came down past his knees.

Dash paused at the end of the table. All eyes in the room were on him. Freshmen, sophomores, professors stared. It was as if the king had finally arrived after we had all traveled miles to see him speak.

"It's official, my friends," Dash announced, spreading his arms wide. "We are throwing a party."

Instantly a murmur rushed across the room, like a ripple rushing outward and splashing against the far walls before making its way back again. Two seconds later, the caf was alive with chatter.

"Now that's more like it," Noelle said, brightening considerably.

"A party?" Taylor squeaked.

"For what?" Natasha asked.

"For Thomas," Gage said. "To, you know, honor his memory and shit."

"Very eloquent, Gage," Whit scolded.

"Excuse me, Master Webster," Gage said, putting on a stuffy New England accent. He placed his hand flat on his chest and raised his nose. "I intended *not* to offend."

Whit blushed and Gage cackled, grabbing a carrot stick from Ariana's plate and crunching into it. Josh, meanwhile, slid in behind me and sat down on Taylor's other side. He didn't look as psyched about the announcement as his friends were.

"Do you really think that's appropriate?" Natasha said, looking meaningfully at me. I loved it when someone else said what I was thinking so that I didn't have to. Natasha had another level of depth that the rest of my friends didn't seem to possess, an ability to imagine what it might be like if the person *she* loved had been found dead off campus. How that might feel. I suspected that Noelle had not bothered to try to empathize with me by imagining Dash six feet under. Doing that would be too unpleasant for the Golden Goddess of Easton.

"Ah, the moral center speaks," Noelle announced. She folded her hands under her chin and looked at Natasha, enraptured. "Do tell us, Mrs. Bush. What is our repression of the day?"

The guys all laughed. Natasha's eyes narrowed into thin slits of hatred. "I'm just saying that maybe not everyone at this school will see death as a reason to party."

"Well, then, they're assbags," Gage said.

"We already got permission from the dean," Dash told us, rubbing his hands together, as if that put an end to Natasha's argument. "We're going to do it the night before Thanksgiving break and make it totally cheesy and cool. Like some kind of Midwest prom or something."

"That's hilarious," Gage said, cracking up.

"Thomas would have loved that," Ariana said.

I looked at her. She had always hated Thomas. Had been the first to warn me away from him. How would she know what he would or wouldn't have loved?

"Think we could smuggle in some strippers?" Gage asked. "Now *that* Thomas would have loved."

My body heat peaked, and I noticed everyone glancing at me to note my reaction. I tried not to have one.

"Coolidge, you are so crass," Natasha said.

"Crenshaw, why don't you and Whittaker get together and spawn already?" Gage suggested. "You could pop out the first mixed-race Republican in America."

Whit scoffed. Natasha narrowed her eyes. "Know what I like most about you, Coolidge?" Natasha said. "You're so ignorant, you think it's something to be proud of."

"You know you love me," Gage replied.

"Enough already. Can we get back to the party now?" Dash said.

"I think it's exactly what we need," Noelle said.

"Exactly," Dash agreed. "Get everyone out of this freakin'

morbid state. It's really bringing me the hell down. And personally, I don't think Pearson would appreciate it."

"He *was* always up for a good party," Kiran said with a thoughtful frown.

"Please. You just want another excuse to get drunk," Noelle joked.

"What do you think, Reed?" Ariana asked me.

I have to say, part of me was touched that any of these people considered anything to be my call. But I supposed that was what happened when you were the girlfriend of the person who had infamously, mysteriously, died. To these people I was practically a widow.

Unfortunately, I found myself unable to process anything. This, like everything else that came my way these days, was just too much for me to handle. What would everyone think? How could I possibly handle a celebration? Could this really be up to me?

Everyone was staring at me. Desperate, I glanced at Josh. "What do you say? Are you ready to party?"

He shrugged. "Might not be the worst idea. If it helps people, you know, move on."

He held my gaze for a moment and I knew he wasn't just thinking about "people." He was thinking about me. He wanted *me* to move on. With him? A skitter of excitement traced its way through the lumps of pain, guilt, and fear in my chest. And, just like that, I had something else I couldn't wrap my brain around.

"I think it's a great idea," I said, forcing a smile. "You guys are right. All this drama isn't very Thomas. Or . . . wasn't."

"Good. Then it's a go," Dash said, pulling a chair up from another table to sit at the head of ours. "And who knows? Maybe by then they'll catch the bastard who did this and we'll really have something to celebrate."

Taylor snorted, and by the time I turned to look at her, tears were already streaming down her face.

"God, Taylor," Noelle said. "Pop a Prozac and get over it already. Like Hollis said, it's time to move on."

Taylor winced at Noelle's words and my heart went out to her. I reached out to pat her back, but she jumped up before I could touch her.

"I have to go to the nurse," she said.

She fumbled to get her bag strap off the back of her chair and knocked it over in the process, causing a huge clatter in the otherwise silent room. Everyone once again looked at us, and Taylor was mortified. She ducked her head and ran, her now ever-present tissue covering her nose.

"What is her deal lately?" Natasha asked.

Noelle, Ariana, and Kiran all exchanged a look. Like they knew something we didn't—which they usually did. Then they turned their attention back to their food. I sat back in my chair, recalling something Constance had said about Taylor a few weeks back when Thomas had first gone missing. The police had been routinely interviewing all the students, and Constance had told me that that Taylor had come out of her meeting in tears. It had seemed odd, so Constance had speculated that maybe Taylor had a crush on Thomas.

The thought, at the time, had made me laugh, because I had chalked the whole Taylor-in-tears thing up to a rumor. But now I wasn't so sure. Considering the way Taylor had been acting since the funeral, it certainly seemed possible that Thomas had meant more to her than I had thought.

On Halloween night, the Billings Girls had assured me there would no longer be any secrets between us. Apparently, they were already taking liberties with that promise.

MURDERED

Early the following week, I was sat across from Noelle in the library, pretending to read *The Grapes of Wrath.* I had read it back in eighth grade during my English teacher's spring reading challenge (which I had won by a landslide), so I technically didn't need to be reading it again. I really should have been studying for my French exam or doing my biology lab, but since I was unable to concentrate on anything for more than five seconds at a time, I figured I'd go with something I had already read. Under the table, my leg jumped up and down as if it were trying to free itself from my torso.

If I didn't flunk out of this place before Christmas, it would be a miracle.

The library was deathly silent aside from the occasional sound of a book spine cracking or a pencil scratching against paper. Back home, our library was full of giggles and whispers and table-hockey games. It was a place for kids to waste their study hall periods gossiping and being generally stupid. At Easton the library was a place to work. When I'd first arrived, this phenomenon had inflated me with a kind of intellectual pride. I was at an actual institution of serious learning. I was a scholar. Today, the silence threatened to kill me. It made it far too easy for my brain to wander to other things.

"I'm going to grab a bottle of water," Noelle said, pulling out her Gucci wallet. "You want anything?"

They didn't have fountains here at Easton. Just Evian vending machines.

"No, thanks," I said.

It still threw me a bit that she was going to get her own stuff now instead of ordering me to go. That she was actually asking what *she* could do for *me*. I should have taken advantage of it—and would have—if stuff like that had even been a remote priority anymore. It didn't seem like it ever would be again.

Noelle turned and sauntered off toward the bathroom alcove, where the machines hummed away. As soon as she was gone, I heard feet pounding on the carpeted floor and looked up. Everyone, in fact, looked up. Lorna Gross came bumbling into view and raced right over to a tableful of sophomores off to my left. Her frizzy hair was triangular, and a few strands stuck to the sheen of sweat on her face. She whispered something breathlessly, spitting all over her friends' books.

Suddenly, everyone was looking at me. Constance, Missy, Diana Waters. Kiki Rosen popped the earbuds out of her ears and turned off her iPod. I felt as if a huge tidal wave were hovering behind me and everyone was just watching it, waiting for it to plunge down on me and sweep me away.

"What?" I said loudly.

Constance looked at the others, then braced her hand on the back of her chair as she reluctantly got up. She walked over and sat down next to me, leaning in so that no one might overhear. I gripped my book in both hands until the pads of my fingertips hurt.

"Reed, they arrested someone," Constance said calmly, soothingly. "Some guy from town named Rick DeLea or something?"

My throat constricted. My heart constricted. My lower stomach tightened into a knot. Suddenly, Constance felt very far away. Everything and everyone seemed to shrink into the background, and all there was in the world was this:

Thomas had been murdered. Thomas had been *murdered*.

So Noelle had been right. So that townie dealer scum that she and Josh had known about, but whom I had never heard of, had killed him.

So . . . so . . . so . . .

"They're saying he was Thomas's middleman or something?" Constance said, her brow coming together and rearranging her freckles.

I nodded mutely. There was no way I could speak.

Missy Thurber got up and strode over to us, Lorna at her side. "Well, well. Guess you won't be milking the tragic heroine thing much longer."

"Shut up, Missy," Constance said, then looked shocked at herself.

"What? I'm just saying. Thomas Pearson wasn't the innocent victim of some twisted anti-prep-school crime. He was just murdered in the middle of a drug deal gone awry. Like some common criminal." Missy leaned into the table and looked me in the eye. "I think that knocks you down a few pegs."

I hardly heard a thing she said. All I could hear, all I could see, was one word: *murdered.* The word I had been avoiding for days. *Murdered.*

Thomas Pearson was murdered.

Hot. No air. I needed air. I squirmed, pulling the turtleneck on my sweater away from my prickling skin.

"They said they found drug paraphernalia and a wad of cash near the body," Missy continued. "Guess somebody had an issue with their *dealer.*"

Someone moved in behind me. Lorna took an uncertain step backward. Missy's face lost all its mirth. She stood up straight.

Noelle placed her water and wallet on the table in front of me, leaned forward past my shoulder, and squinted at Missy. She tilted her head deliberately to one side, then the other, as if trying to see something better. No one moved. No one dared say a word.

"Huh," Noelle said.

"What?" Missy blurted tremulously.

Noelle frowned and rounded her shoulders. "I always wondered if you could actually see through those cavernous nostrils to China, but everything's pretty much obscured by the forest of nasal hair."

Someone snorted. Missy's hand flew up to cover her nose.

"It's Missy Thurber, right?" Noelle said. "Your mother and sister were in Billings?"

Missy was a marble-white statue of her former self.

"Well, thanks, Missy. You just inspired me to abolish that archaic little Billings rule about automatic admission for legacies," Noelle said. "Have fun in Dayton House next year. I hear they've just about cleaned up that nasty rat problem."

Missy's mouth hung open so wide I could have stuffed my fist into it. She let out a strangled noise as she turned on her heel and ran away, fingers still covering her nose. Lorna scurried after her, seeing her own shot at Billings-by-association go up in smoke. It would have been a perfect moment, if those images of Thomas lying dead and bloody with bags of pills and powder all around him would have just stopped assaulting me.

The imagination is a horrible thing.

"Are you okay?" Noelle asked me, stepping into my line of vision.

"I don't know," I said.

"Maybe you should go lie down or something," Constance suggested.

"Good idea," Noelle put in.

Constance turned pink with pleasure.

"Come on," Noelle said as she quickly packed up my stuff and hers. "Let's get you back to Billings."

Constance and I stood up, and Noelle stayed close to my side as we headed for the front door. Somehow, I managed to put one foot in front of the other, but I was glad there were no obstacles in front of me. I was so stunned I would have walked into a rhino if it had stepped into my path.

"It's going to be okay, Reed," Noelle told me. She seemed energized. Vehement. "It is. At least they caught the guy, right? It's finally over. That bastard is going down."

She pushed open the door and a gust of cold air hit me square in the face. I gasped for breath and looked up at the stars that blanketed the November sky.

At least they caught the guy. That bastard is going down.

Maybe someday those words would mean what Noelle wanted them to mean, but for now they only meant one thing. Thomas didn't have to die. Someone had decided to kill him.

And suddenly, the anger was back.

OLD FRIENDS

I stared out the front window of Billings the next morning, waiting for Ariana and Taylor to finish getting ready. Tiny droplets of rain dotted the glistening windowpane and the sky was overcast, a perfect backdrop for my heavy mood. I took a deep breath and released it slowly through my lips, marveling at how the campus beyond still managed to look beautiful to me even at this time of year, even in this state of mind. It was already mid-November, but the grass was still green and clipped and the evergreen shrubs perfectly shaped. Overnight, beads of water had frozen along the leafless limbs of the trees at the end of the walk, forming a canopy of diamonds. Back home there would be nothing but brown and gray. Dead grass, dead plants, piles of soaked and rotting leaves the public service had neglected to pick up. November was one of Croton's ugliest months of the year. Nothing was ever ugly at Easton. Even in the wake of murder.

There was a bustling on the stairs, and I turned to find Ariana and Taylor coming toward me, Ariana pulling on her pristine white calfskin gloves. "Ready?" she asked, looking positively bright-eyed.

"Ready."

The moment we walked outside I was nearly knocked over by a gust of wind and a smattering of drizzle. Ariana and Taylor stepped out of Billings behind me and instinctively huddled close.

"I need coffee," I mumbled, buttoning the top button on my new Lands' End wool coat, which my father had ordered and had shipped directly to me. It was much more practical and boxy than any of the designer coats the other Billings Girls had hanging in their closets, but at least it was warm.

"I need oatmeal," Taylor added.

She was looking a bit more like herself today. Her blond curls danced around her face, and she had gotten some color back in her skin. Although that might have just been the wind.

"So, you're going to eat today?" Ariana asked, tucking her arm through mine as we speed-walked across campus, our shoes clip-clopping on the wet stone path. "Both of you?"

"I'll give it a try," I said.

The truth was, my appetite had yet to return. The only reason I was in such a rush to get to the cafeteria was to see if there was any more news, if anyone had heard anything about this Rick character. If worse came to worst, I might even seek out Walt Whittaker for a tête-à-tête, as awkward as that would be. Whit's and my dating experiment had only imploded a little over a week ago, the very night Thomas was found, but Whit also had a blood connection to the powers that be at Easton. His grandmother was on the board of directors, which meant that I might just have to suck it up and talk to him.

We were about to turn up the short path to the cafeteria when I saw someone out of the corner of my eye. I paused and my pulse started to race, warming my skin. Detective Hauer. Out for his morning stroll, even in this weather. If there was one person who could tell me more than even Whit could, it was Hauer.

I stopped and waited for him to join us.

"Good morning, ladies," he said with a kind smile, though his brown eyes looked sad and tired. His black trench coat was stretched over his stocky frame, the belt barely tying at the waist. "Brisk one."

"Yes, Detective. It certainly is," Ariana said, her southern manners kicking in.

"How are you today, Reed?" he asked me.

I don't know why I grew warm at his singling me out. We had met on the quad before, just like this, except I had been alone at the time. Plus he had interviewed me with the chief just yesterday. We were practically old friends.

"Is it true, Detective?" I asked. I felt a rush of nauseating excitement and dread at being able to pose the question. Finally. "Did they really arrest that guy? Did he do it?"

He lifted his head slightly and studied me for a moment before answering. "We do have a suspect in custody, yes. But as to whether or not he had anything to do with your friend's death, we're not sure yet. He's still being questioned."

"But if you brought him in, you must have had a good reason," Ariana said.

"There was compelling evidence, yes," the detective said.

"What does that mean?" I asked.

"Just that he's a suspect, that's all," the detective told me gently. "I know how close you were with Thomas, Reed. I didn't have a chance to tell you yesterday, but I wanted you to know how sorry I am for your loss."

Ariana's grip on my arm tightened. Like that last moment in the blood pressure sleeve when you think the doctor might be taking the thing a pump or ten too far just to see if you'll pop. The twisting in the back of my throat returned. I tried to swallow but couldn't, and my eyes instantly watered.

"I promise I'll let you know as soon as we know anything for sure," he told me.

I nodded. I wanted to thank him, but I knew I had to wait for this latest wave of misery to pass.

"Thank you, Detective," Ariana said, easing her death grip slightly. "Come on, girls. Let's get inside before we freeze."

She really was becoming more like a mother every day. And I couldn't have been more grateful for it. If it hadn't been for her tugging on my arm, I might have stood there in the cold all day.

"Ladies," the detective said, stepping back.

"Bye," I heard myself say.

Ariana led us over to the door and opened it for us, waiting for Taylor and me to go through first. The warmth of the heated cafeteria enveloped me, and I breathed for the first time in what felt like hours.

"There. See?" Ariana said, facing me and Taylor. She slipped out of her light blue cashmere coat and folded it over her arm. "Don't you feel better now? Don't you *both* feel better?"

I looked at Taylor and she blew out a sigh, smiling slightly. It was the first smile I had seen on her since the Saturday night when we had all been in New York City, partying like the carefree idiots we'd been at the time.

"Yeah. Definitely," Taylor said, unbuttoning her plaid coat.

"Definitely," I echoed.

Now I just had to start believing it.

RESIGNED

Our grades arrived.

Grades. I had forgotten the quarter was ending. But there it was, in my mailbox in the hallway outside the school store: a crisp, cream envelope standing at an angle right up against the window. I could see hundreds of others just like it in hundreds of other mailboxes. A few feet away, a group of dizzy freshmen ripped theirs open and compared their contents. They giggled in triumph and groaned in dismay. My fingers itched to work my combination, but my fight-or-flight reflex kicked into high gear. I couldn't deal with this. Not right now. I turned around and walked out into the cold.

As soon as the door closed behind me I felt lighter somehow, empowered. I'd finally taken control of something, however small. I knew I'd have to look inside that envelope, but for now I was resolved to remain ignorant. And it felt good.

That night, I was determined to actually study. Whatever those grades were, I was going to improve upon them in the second semester. This was exactly what I needed to get over Thomas. I would become a brain. An overachiever. I would throw myself into my work and forget about everything else. I walked determinedly into the library with my history book and my notebook and a new pen. I was going to take notes for the next day's quiz, using the advice Taylor had given me at the beginning of the year. All I had to do was copy the first and last sentence of every paragraph. That was where Mr. Barber always got his quiz questions. It was busy-work. If I couldn't handle even that, I was in big trouble.

Every person I strode by stopped what they were doing to watch me go, and I felt my shoulder muscles coil, but I kept my focus dead ahead. I was tired of everyone staring at me. Whispering about me. Asking me if I was okay. But how could I blame them? In the past couple of weeks I had become a walking catastrophe. Spacing out in class. Staring at nothing in the library. Sleeping until the very last moment possible because usually those last twenty minutes were the only sleep I got. One morning I was so out of it that I was halfway across the quad before I realized I was wearing two different shoes. At Easton, that was akin to showing up naked.

Well, as of now, that was all going to change. I had to stop waiting for one of those fairy-tale godmother people to come along and hit me with a wand to the head to make me forget everything. It was up to me now.

In the center of the library, two guys from Drake House, one of the less appealing guys' dorms (nicknamed "Dreck House"), sat at the end of a long table. Neither of them looked up when I passed.

I liked them already. I sat down at the far side and opened my book.

Okay. Here we go. Work time.

"Reed?"

I blinked a couple of dozen times. My eyes stung. Finally they focused on Josh, who was sitting down across from me. I felt like I'd just been shaken awake. I glanced at my watch. Half an hour had passed. My notebook was blank.

"Hey," he said. He looked wary as he placed his messenger bag down on top of the table. "Are you okay?"

"I'm *fine,*" I said through my teeth. "I just wish people would stop asking me that."

Josh raised his hands. "Sorry."

I felt instantly guilty. I couldn't start snapping at my friends now. If I lost them too, I would have nothing at all. Something between a sigh and a groan parted my lips.

"No. *I'm* sorry." I crossed my arms over my notebook and my forehead hit my wrist. "I didn't mean to tear your head off," I said into the table.

"It's okay," Josh whispered sincerely. "What's going on?"

I felt his finger touch my pinky. It warmed me all over. One millimeter of skin on skin, and my whole body reacted. What would Thomas have thought? Was he watching me right now? Was that even possible? Did he know I was having warm and fuzzy feelings for one of his best friends? I squeezed my eyes closed and shook my head, trying to shake the thoughts out.

It wasn't fair. It wasn't. Nothing was fair.

"Reed?" His voice took on a serious, concerned tone that set every inch of me vibrating.

With a sigh I lifted my head enough so that my chin was now on my notebook. I looked up at him pathetically. I wished he would just hug me. Somehow I felt that if I could find myself in Josh's arms—just held there in his arms—I could start to feel okay. But how could I do that? How could either of us do that?

"I just wish I could get out of my head," I told him after a long moment. "It's unlivable in here."

Josh smirked. He leaned forward, bringing his face close to the table, so close to mine I could see every light freckle across his nose. "I might have an idea of how you can do that, if you're interested," he said, with a mischievous glint in his normally glint-free eyes.

Well. That was foreboding.

I sat up straight. "If you're talking about pot or something, I'm not interested," I said, adjusting my books as if I was actually going to study. "Considering," I added pointedly.

"It's not drugs, Reed. Come on," Josh said, sitting up as well. "How idiotic do you think I am?"

I blinked. A blush moved in from behind my ears, warming my face all the way to my nose. So this was what shame felt like.

"Then what is it?" I asked.

"It's better," he said.

I looked down at the blank pages in my notebook and took a deep breath. "I'm in."

ENOUGH DAMAGE

My heart was pounding so loudly in my ears I had a feeling they would be ringing later. I hadn't been in Ketlar for weeks. Not since Thomas was still alive. Not since he had brought me here to have sex.

Make love.

Use me?

I had no idea anymore. And now I'd never be able to ask him. Whatever it had been, being so close to the place where it had happened was conjuring several physical reactions.

Nausea. Shaky knees. Headache. Watery eyes. I was one big side effect.

"Come on," Josh half-whispered the moment the elevator doors slid open.

It took a lot of effort for me to move. I followed him out into the hallway and toward the common room. I knew I should be excited and curious about what, exactly, Josh had in mind, but ghosts of memories were crowding out any immediate concerns. Visions of

Thomas sprawled out on the leather couch. Playing video games on the flat screen with his friends. Raucous laughter and cheers and jeers.

There was none of it now. The place was dead. It smelled antiseptic, as if someone had come in and bleached the walls. The TV was gray and the game console had been stashed underneath in the cabinet. One guy I didn't know read at the table in the corner by the light of a dim lamp.

It was as if all the life had gone out of Ketlar along with Thomas.

Josh quickly crossed the common room—the only place in the dorm where I was legally permitted to be (not that I had heeded that rule in the past)—and headed into the far hallway. Suddenly I knew where he was taking me. To his room. Thomas's room.

"Uh, I don't think this is the best idea," I said.

"We're not gonna get caught," Josh whispered, taking my hand, just as Thomas had taken my hand right here in this place not all that long ago. "Mr. Cross has been in meetings practically twenty-four/seven since they found Thomas."

I tripped forward as he tugged me. My murky brain tried to find the words to tell him that the last place on Earth I wanted to be was Thomas's room, but we were already in the hall. My breath caught. There it was, the closed door looming up on the left like a creature from hell that could swallow me whole. Inside that room were all of Thomas's things. The clothes that still smelled like him. The books he always stacked next to his desk. The bed that we . . . that we . . . that—

I opened my mouth to say something. Anything. I could *not* go in there.

And then we were walking past it.

Josh opened the door at the very end of the hallway. "Here we go."

"What? But I thought—"

I stepped into the tiniest room I had ever seen, barely larger than a Billings closet. The walls were bare, but there were paint splatters everywhere, in every color of the rainbow. I recognized Josh's bedspread from his old room. The bed, desk, and dresser had all been pushed up against one wall so that three easels could be set up along the other. The third was dominated by a tall, slim window. Next to the door was a skinny closet jammed with clothing.

"They moved me here the week after the funeral, after they inspected all my stuff for clues or whatever," Josh said, dropping his messenger bag on his bed. "My old room is a crime scene now."

"Oh. God. I didn't even think of that."

"I know," Josh said, his eyes dark. "I hate it. It's like, how much can one person go through? It's like I—" He stopped himself mid-ramble, as if biting his tongue, and glanced at me. "It just sucks."

"Yeah," I said. I had no idea what else to say.

He moved over to the corner where there was a paint-speckled box with a handle on top. He lifted it with one hand and used the side of it to shove some papers and pens on his desk aside so that he could set it down. Watching him, I felt like I could see what he had been like as a little kid. Somehow he had gotten smaller.

More vulnerable. And I realized, suddenly, how selfish I had been.

"Josh, I'm so sorry," I said, dropping down on his bed. I shrugged out of my coat and laid it aside. "Everyone keeps asking me how I am, but I never asked you . . . are *you* okay?"

Josh blew out a breath through his nose. "Yeah. I guess," he said. "The whole thing is surreal, but . . . what am I going to do, you know?"

I stared at him. "Most of the time you seem so normal. How are you dealing with all this?"

He looked down. Shuffled his feet. "I have my ways."

Ooooohkay.

"Like what?"

"That's why I brought you here," he said. He popped open the box and lifted out a few paintbrushes. "I'm going to show you one of them."

He slipped an iPod from his jacket pocket and placed it in its speaker system on his desk. One hit of one button, and suddenly the room was filled with screeching guitar. I had to concentrate to keep from wincing.

"What're you doing?" I shouted.

"Helping you get out of your head!" Josh moved over to the first easel and opened up a few jars of paint that were sitting in the attached tray. Then he did the same at the second easel. He turned and handed me a few of the brushes. I stared at them, confused. Did he expect me to *paint*?

Josh lifted one of the jars from the tray and walked to the center of the small room. He dipped one of his larger brushes into the jar.

"This is what I do when my headspace becomes . . . unlivable," he told me.

Then he dipped the brush in the paint, came out with a big glob, and flung it at the canvas. Half the paint hit the canvas—a huge, red slash across the stark white. The other half of the paint hit the wall. Now I understood where the splatters had come from.

"Try it," Josh shouted.

"Are you insane?" I asked. His eyes flashed at me and something inside of me paused. Hesitated. I looked around. "I mean, they're gonna freak when they see what you're doing to this place."

"They don't care!" Josh smiled and shrugged and I wondered if I'd imagined the sudden darkness I'd thought I'd seen. "I'm the poor, pathetic roommate of the dead guy." He paused for a moment and his expression shifted, as if he'd just realized how callous he'd sounded. "No one cares what I do," he added.

My heart pounded in sympathy for him. "That's not true."

He focused on me as if suddenly remembering I was there. "No! I don't mean literally. I just mean . . . forget it. Come on, Reed. Try this! I swear it'll help."

He took my hand and pressed a brush into it. My breath started to race at his nearness and his excitement. Josh was energized. I craved that. I craved the idea of feeling anything even remotely positive. I pushed myself up and grabbed a jar of blue paint. I dipped the brush into it and looked at Josh.

"Now fling it," he instructed.

I grinned. Suddenly I couldn't help it. Being with Josh made me grin. There it was. So what if it was disloyal? If it was cruel? Right then, I just wanted to keep smiling. So I lifted my arm and flung. Most of my paint hit the wall. The easel only took a drop. Somehow the rest of it splashed Josh in the face.

I took one look at him and cracked up laughing. It felt so, so good to laugh. Josh slowly wiped the paint from his nose with his fingertips, making a nice, wide smear across his cheek.

"Oh my God! You're right! I *do* feel better," I said.

It hurt to laugh, like I was using a muscle that hadn't been exercised in too long. Josh turned around and I was hit in the face with a smattering of green. Kid was so quick I never even saw it coming.

"Touché," I said, wiping my forehead.

I grabbed another vat of paint and hit him again. He hit me with a blob of red right in the center of my black sweater. I screeched and doused him in yellow. Suddenly we were both laughing and attacking. Before I knew it, Josh was swiping at me with a brush, making random slashes on my clothes. I had paint in my hair, on my shoes, all over my favorite jeans. But I didn't even care. This was the best time I had had in days. The lightest I had felt since Thomas's funeral. Even on my nonbudget, I could sacrifice some clothing for that.

Josh came at me with a brush. I straight-armed his shoulder and held him back, wheezing for breath. He grabbed my waist, twisted me around. I escaped his grasp and headed for the wall.

Josh was everywhere. His hands, his fingers, his breath, his laughter, his weight. It was all one blur, and all of it sent my heart rate skyrocketing.

He was going to grab me and kiss me. Every inch of me was throbbing and I knew he felt it too. He had to. I gripped the sleeve of his shirt and didn't let go. Our bodies were pressed together as the vertical wrestling match started to wane. I could feel his breath on my neck as I slowly straightened up. I looked him in the eye.

Come on. Do it. Please. I just want to keep this feeling going. I don't want to go back. I don't want to go back. . . .

"I think you'd look good in purple," Josh said huskily, teasingly, backing me toward the wall. "What do you think?"

My stomach hurt from laughing and I was out of breath. "Don't. Don't you dare," I said, watching the brush in his hand.

Josh, of course, kept coming.

"Reed, hold still! You have to let an artist do his work!"

He lifted the brush.

"Josh! No! Come on!" I laughed, pressing my hands into his chest. "Haven't you done enough damage already?"

Josh hovered inches from me, taunting me with the paint. Aside from the original blue streak, he had flecks of green and yellow in his hair and a smatter of black across his cheek. He looked me in the eye and grinned.

My heart missed a beat. Then another. I stared at his paint-spattered lips. His breath grew heavier as he stepped even closer. My skin tingled with warmth.

Do it. Please. Just kiss me.

His eyes traveled down to my lips. I could already feel them buzzing. I looked him in the eye.

Please, Josh. Please.

Suddenly, he blinked and backed off. Everything inside of me nose-dived, so fast I almost physically fell over. "You're right," he said. "Enough damage for one night."

My face burned with humiliation. There was no way he didn't know what I'd been thinking. I'd practically said the word *please* out loud. I had to get out of here. Now. I cleared my throat and wiped my hands on my jeans, making them even messier. My coat and bag seemed, miraculously, unscathed, but I couldn't pick them up in my current state.

"I need a bathroom," I blurted.

"Down the hall on the right."

Josh couldn't even look at me.

"Right. I remember."

After struggling with the door handle with my paint-covered hands I finally broke free and raced down the hall, as if I could somehow leave what had just almost happened behind me. Shoving my way into the bathroom, I startled a Ketlar guy who was standing right opposite the door. I braced my hands on the white sink. My reflection was frightening—matted, sticky hair, multicolored swirls all over my face—but I didn't even care. All I could see were my eyes.

The eyes of a girl who had just tried to seduce her dead boyfriend's roommate.

NOT TO BE SAD

I skipped breakfast the next day. I couldn't face Josh. Instead, I stood in the shower for thirty minutes, letting the hot water scorch my skin, wishing it could burn away all feeling. When Natasha knocked on the door and asked if I was coming, I told her I needed to be alone. She left, no questions asked. One of the benefits of being the widow.

The quad was peaceful when I emerged, cuddled into my favorite white cotton sweater—which I had been wearing almost every day lately—and buttoning up my coat. I expected to take a slow, solitary stroll to morning services, but when I looked up, Constance was just coming out the back door of Bradwell. She grinned in surprise.

"Hey! What are you doing out here?" she asked as we turned together up the path that led past Mitchell Hall and the cafeteria to the chapel.

"Running late," I said. "You?"

"Oh, my mom called," Constance said, rolling her eyes.

"My little brother Trey got chicken pox and now Carla, the nanny, has it, too, so my mom has basically gone to the zoo. She's babbling about vaccination shots and surgical masks and the end of the world. Have I mentioned that my mother is not all there?"

I smirked. Constance was always good for a distraction.

"What's your mom like?" she asked innocently.

I bit my tongue against the flash of anger that always took over at any thought of my mother. It was amazing how powerful it was. But I didn't want to bite her head off or say something dismissive. I had done that to her before in response to one of her naive questions, and I was trying to better myself.

"Let's just say she went to the zoo a long time ago and she's still there, feeding the monkeys," I said.

Constance's brows knit, but then she laughed. "You're too funny, Reed."

"I try," I said flatly.

We came around the corner and my stomach attempted to drop out of my body. Josh was waiting against the chapel wall. He stepped away when he saw us. So, waiting for me.

"Hey," he said tentatively.

"Hey."

I looked at Constance. Constance looked at me. Like she was trying to process something. Was my guilt written all over my face, or was the warmth in the air that I felt around Josh now palpable to everyone else as well?

"You missed breakfast," he said knowingly.

"Observant," I replied. Because he had to say it knowingly. Like he was so smart and had me all figured out.

"Can I talk to you?" Josh asked, one hand in his pocket, the other cradling his books at his hip. He was wearing an open coat over a battered corduroy jacket over a band T-shirt, and his jeans were frayed at the cuffs.

"Sure."

"I'll see you in there," Constance told me. She looked at me over her shoulder before disappearing inside the chapel. Like she didn't recognize me.

"What's up?" I asked.

Josh tilted his head away from the door, where students from the cafeteria were hustling by, eager to get back into the warmth of the indoors. I followed him. My pulse was causing my skin to throb. Was he going to mention last night? Our aborted kiss? Was he going to tell me it was wrong? That he didn't want to be around me anymore? He stopped and turned to face me.

"So, my brother, Lynn, and his girlfriend, Gia, are coming up from Yale tomorrow to check up on me," he said.

Hello, whiplash. Both the words and the casual tone in which they were said were so unexpected it took my brain a second to catch up.

"Okay," I said brilliantly.

"See, my parents are in Germany and they're all worried after what happened, so they're sending out a posse, basically," Josh said. "We're probably going to go up to Boston to hang out for the day, so I was wondering if you wanted to come."

The invitation hung in the air. Around us students talked and milled and laughed. Each day since the funeral the student body had reanimated a bit more. They were almost back up to normal pitch now. Just a couple weeks later.

"So. Do you?" Josh prompted.

"Want to come to Boston?" I asked.

"Yeah."

"With you and your brother and your brother's girlfriend."

Sounded like a double date to me. Was that what it was intended to sound like?

"Yeah," Josh said, confused. "Was that not clear?"

I smiled and looked down at my shoes. Why did he have to be so cute?

"We'll do something fun," Josh said, nudging my arm with his books. "I think it'll be good, you know? To get out of here . . . do something different . . . ?"

The very thought sent a rush of excitement through me. Followed by a crippling stab of Thomas-related guilt. What was I supposed to do here? What? Stay true to the memory of my murdered boyfriend, or start trying to get on with my life?

I knew what Noelle and Ariana would say. That there was no point in wallowing, and here Josh was, offering me one day of carefree fun. One day to not be sad.

And, okay, if I was being honest, one day to figure out what the hell there was between us.

"Okay," I said finally, lifting my shoulders. "Sure. Why not?"

Josh grinned and my heart stopped. Just like that.

Good decision, Reed. Good decision.

FIRSTS

There were no lights on in the chapel. The November sun cast a dull glow on the room, and all the faces appeared muted and blurred at the edges, like an impressionist painting come to life. I slid into the pew and sat between Constance and Diana. The moment my butt hit the hard wood, the back doors closed. Darker still.

"What's going on?" I asked. A sliver of irrational fear raced down my spine.

"It's firsts," Diana whispered, as the entire room hushed.

"Guess not even a murder investigation can stop them from whipping out the jackets," someone behind me muttered bitterly.

Okay. That sentence made zero sense. "What's 'firsts'?"

"Shhhhh!"

Just like on the very first day of school, two freshmen boys stepped out from the shadows and lit the lanterns at the front of the chapel. We were all bathed in their warm, cozy, glow. Dean Marcus rose from his chair and stood at the podium. He looked around at all of us in an appraising way.

"Tradition, honor, excellence," he intoned.

"Tradition, honor, excellence," we all echoed.

"Students, today is a day of celebration," the dean announced, his strong, weighty voice echoing off the stone walls. "We here at this hallowed academy will not allow recent events, as terrible as they may be, to deter us from our ultimate goal. We will continue to strive for excellence in every facet of our lives. Today I have the pleasure of announcing to you the names of those students who have achieved first honors for the first semester of our academic year."

"Here, here!" one of the professors cheered with a raised fist, earning a round of applause from the hall.

"As always, I will start with the freshman class. When I call your name, please come up and receive your founders' jacket," the dean said. For the first time in days, I saw a hint of a smile on his face. The man vibed on tradition. "From the freshman class, the students who have received the highest all-around marks this first semester are . . . April Park and Carson Levere."

As everyone around me applauded, I leaned toward Diana's ear. "Founders' jacket?"

"The guy and the girl from each class who get the highest GPA get to wear founders' jackets all day," Diana said as she clapped. Onstage, the dean was lifting a blue blazer with the Easton crest on the pocket onto April Park's shoulders. "It's this huge honor. People around here would kill to wear that jacket."

Sure enough, April's face shone and her eyes brimmed with

tears. She touched the sleeve of her jacket with her fingertips as if it were made from spun gold. You could tell she was just aching to call her parents right then and there. Maybe they'd give her a pony. A quick survey of the room revealed that almost every student of any merit was sitting forward in his or her seat, salivating. This was serious business.

April and Carson stood aside. Instantly, the applause halted.

"From the sophomore class," Dean Marcus continued, glancing at a page on the podium. Suddenly I wished I had opened my mailbox and gotten my grades. Not that I had any sort of shot at this, but I would have loved to have known for sure that there was zero chance my name would be called. "Kiki Rosen and Corey Snow."

"Omigod! Kiki!" Diana exclaimed, elbowing her roommate.

At first I thought Kiki hadn't heard, that her music was deafening her as always. But then she calmly removed her earbuds and stood up, looking totally and completely unaffected. It wasn't until the jacket was safely on her body that she finally busted out in a grin. Honestly, in that moment, I was jealous. And in the next I marveled at how quickly something like that could take hold. And the next, how I was actually thinking about something other than Thomas.

Amazing, the power Easton could have.

"Did you know she was that smart?" Constance asked us.

"No! Maybe she has our lessons on constant loop on her iPod," Diana said, baffled.

"From the junior class," the dean continued. "Well, here's no surprise. Taylor Bell and Lance Reagan."

I cheered extra loud for Taylor, but as she walked past us, she hid behind her hair and kept her eyes trained on the floor. My spirits slumped along with her shoulders. I wished I could see her bounding up there all bubbly and excited. I missed the Taylor I'd met back in September.

"And finally, from the senior class . . ." Dean Marcus announced.

"Noelle Lange and Dash McCafferty," Diana recited with a slight eye roll and smile.

"What?" I said.

"They *always* win," Diana told me. "We're talking four semesters a year since seventh grade. Accept no substitutes."

Shocker.

"Ariana Osgood—"

There was an audible, chapelwide gasp, like we'd all just gone over the top of the highest hill on one massive roller coaster. Every single pair of eyes turned around to gape at Noelle, who was half out of her seat, and at Ariana, who was perched next to her as always, looking stunned. There was an awkward moment of suspended animation before Noelle plopped, more awkwardly than I've ever seen her do anything, back into the pew.

"And Dash McCafferty!" the dean finished.

When Dash got up, he looked deeply confused. Ariana whispered something to Noelle before sliding past her and joining Dash in the aisle. Together, they walked stiffly to the front of the chapel. Anyone who was not watching Ariana was watching Noelle. She kept her eyes trained straight forward, but I could see her jaw clenching.

"What happened?" someone whispered.

"Noelle is going to throw a shit," someone else said.

Up on the stage, the dean lifted the jacket onto Ariana's shoulders. Never had I seen her smile so wide.

A VIBE

"How'd you do?" Constance asked me as we walked out of history class.

"Okay, I think."

I hugged my books to my chest and stepped sideways to get around a couple of the guys in my class. I just wanted out of here. Everywhere I went these days, I wanted out. Then I'd get to wherever I was going next and want out of there, too. At least I hadn't been forced to lie about the quiz. After my encounter with Josh the night before, I had been in a manic state of self-loathing and simultaneous euphoria that had made me more hyper than ten shots of espresso. With my desk light on half the night I had actually managed to study and absorb enough info to squeak by.

Thank God. Because after the head rush of the first-honors ceremony I had run to the post office to grab my grades. All B's. Every last one of them. Except for history. Barber, thanks to my stellar quiz grades, which I had only achieved due to Taylor's advice, had been forced to give me an A. Now that I had one, I thought it might be nice to keep it. Maybe even earn another one somehow next semester. If I could just manage to stop obsessing about other things.

"So . . . what's the deal with you and Josh Hollis?" Constance asked.

"There's no deal with me and Josh," I lied.

I shoved open the door to the stairwell so hard I almost rearranged April Park's face. She scowled at me. Her founders' jacket was obviously lined with bravado. Already she was high on the instant fame.

"Sorry," I said.

Suddenly her face seemed to register who I was and she ducked past me without a word. *Yeah. Billings Girl and Pearson widow trump first honors and founders' jacket, freshman. Keep walking.*

"Are you sure?" Constance asked. "Because . . . it's just I thought you guys had kind of a vibe before and I just thought . . . I don't know. I thought it was weird."

A hot rush of anger zipped through me, severing my nerves.

"You thought it was weird," I said, my fingers curling tightly.

"Because, you know, he was Thomas's roommate and everything," Constance pointed out as we found ourselves on the second floor.

Like I needed that fact to be pointed out.

"Well, there was no vibe, okay?" I snapped. "Maybe you should re-adjust your radar."

Constance's chin drooped, like I'd just snatched away her

lollipop and tossed it in a gutter. I turned on my heel and walked ahead of her. Okay, so maybe I should have bitten my tongue again, but a girl could only take so much. Could I do nothing around here anymore without being questioned? Judged? Here everyone was telling me to get on with my life, but whatever I did, it seemed there were a thousand people watching me and waiting to comment. It was so unfair. I wished everyone would just leave me alone. Didn't they have better things to think about?

I passed by a couple of whispering junior girls and stared stonily ahead, my fingers clenching ever tighter at my sides. I couldn't take being under the microscope for much longer. Something was going to have to give, before I snapped.

ME AND MY ANGER

"Brennan! What the hell are you doing? Pass the ball! *Brennan!*"

I ignored Coach Lisick and streaked down the field, dodging the defenders and faking out one of my teammates so badly she fell on her face. Not my problem. *If you can't keep up, don't bother trying.* The ball was mine.

My body was hot with exertion, but the sweat on my neck and under my hair was cold. It tightened my scalp as a stiff wind blew, but it only made me run harder. With each step I was more in control. Out here no one could stare at me or whisper or point. Out here there was no one but me. Me and my anger. And only one of us was going home alive.

I saw Maddy Sullivan coming at me from the corner of my eye, the red mesh vest she wore over her practice jersey a mere streak. At six feet tall and with one hundred seventy-five pounds of muscle, Maddy could have been a linebacker—or even a pro wrestler, with her rep for playing dirty. I knew she was out for blood just then. My blood.

"Bring it on, bitch," I said through my teeth. I had to take this out on someone. She was as good a candidate as any.

Maddy slammed right into me full force, but I was ready for her. She might as well have hit a brick wall. She stumbled backward, surprised, then came at me again, but this time she did something she had never done before. She went for the ball instead of the body. And she got it. Easily, since I'd been expecting a tackle and had instead gotten a good soccer maneuver.

"Shit," I said under my breath, turning on my heel to chase the ball back the other way. That was my ball. Mine. No one was taking it away from me.

Maddy passed to Bernadette Baskin, who avoided Noelle by passing upfield to Karyn Morris.

"Do I have to do everything around here?" I shouted at the top of my lungs. "They're eating us alive!"

I tore across the field. That was my ball. Mine. I was getting it back. No matter what.

Karyn made the mistake of pausing to assess the defense. I raced up behind her at full speed, turning on the sprint the closer I got. She was just reaching her foot back to pass when I slammed into her from behind, shoving her over with both arms. Karyn let out a surprised sound just before her face slammed into the dirt.

"I'll be taking that," I said, kicking the ball away.

The whistle blew. It shrieked, actually.

"What the hell was that?" Maddy shouted, coming at me with her unusual abundance of testosterone.

"What? That was a clean play!" I shouted back.

"Like hell it was!" Maddy snapped.

Behind me someone helped Karyn up. She coughed dramatically, trying to catch her breath.

"Wuss," I said under my breath.

"What's your problem?" Maddy shouted, bumping my chest. Coach Lisick jogged across the field.

"Maybe you're my problem!" I raged, getting up in Maddy's face.

"Hey! Back off, you two!" Noelle demanded.

She stepped in between me and Maddy and held up her hands. I glared triumphantly at Maddy. Everyone on this field knew whose side Noelle was going to take. I even saw a few of them roll their eyes.

Noelle took a deep breath and looked at me. "Reed, hit the showers. You're done for the day."

My face prickled. Maddy smirked. I think she even grunted.

"What? Noelle!"

"She's right, Brennan," Coach Lisick said. "Go cool off."

"Coach, I'm fine," I argued.

"No, you're not," she told me flatly. "That was your third questionable hit of the day. If this were a game, you would have been red-carded twenty minutes ago. Now I need you to get your ass to the showers before you injure someone. I do have to field a team this weekend, you know."

Someone laughed. Everyone else stared me down or avoided

eye contact completely. Like I was supposed to feel chagrined or sorry.

They had no clue. All I really felt was betrayed. I glared at Noelle as fiercely as humanly possible as I shoved by her and headed for the bleachers. Where the hell did she get off, taking Maddy and Karyn's side? I thought the Billings Girls were supposed to have one another's backs. No matter what.

"Reed!"

She was jogging to catch up with me. I kept walking.

"Reed!"

Her fingers closed around my arm. I yanked it away so quickly her fingernails scraped me through my long-sleeved undershirt.

"What's your problem?"

I whirled on her. "I'm really sorry you didn't get first honors like always, Noelle, but you don't have to take it out on me."

Noelle looked as if she'd just been slapped. For a moment. In the next moment her eyes smoldered with barely suppressed rage. "Don't talk about things you don't understand, glass-licker," she said. That was the first time she'd used my derogatory nickname in weeks. "I'm going to give you a pass on that one because you're clearly out of your mind right now."

I rolled my eyes. "Whatever. Thanks for the support out there."

She stared at me. "We have our last game coming up," she said. "Coach is right. You were going to hurt someone."

"Like you care," I scoffed, and kept walking.

I wasn't making sense. I knew I wasn't. But I was pissed off.

And if she wasn't going to give me something to kick or hit, I didn't want to be there anymore. But Noelle didn't give up that easily. She jogged in front of me, forcing me to stop. Her dark eyes searched mine.

"Reed, if this is about Thomas—"

Instantly all the heat in my body rushed to my face. "I don't want to talk about Thomas anymore!" I shouted.

She didn't even flinch. "Reed, you need to calm down. You need—"

"All I need is for you and everyone else to stop telling me what I need!" I snapped.

This time when I stepped around her and stormed off, she didn't even try to stop me.

KIDNAPPED

I awoke with a jolt. My first thought was *earthquake*. Not that there were many of those in rural Connecticut. Then I heard the whispers. Saw the shadows looming against the white walls. Not an earthquake. Just the Billings Girls.

"What the hell?"

"She's awake. Get the blindfold," Noelle said.

My heart, already in my throat, started to pound there.

"What—"

Someone slipped a silk scarf around my eyes, blocking out the early morning light. The blindfold caught hair and yanked at my scalp.

"Ow!"

"Sorry. Too tight?" Ariana's voice. Sugary sweet. She didn't attempt to loosen the blindfold.

"What are you guys doing?" I asked. My hand flew to the knot at the back of my head. Someone grabbed my wrist and brought it back down.

"Kidnapping you," Kiran replied. "Let's go."

Kidnapping me? *Kidnapping* me? I had thought all the hazing was over. Why couldn't these people just leave me alone? The covers were yanked down and someone forcibly grabbed my ankles, turning me so that my legs shot out over the floor. I reached for the blindfold again. Someone slapped my hand so hard it stung.

"Don't make me get out the handcuffs," Kiran said.

Drawers opened and slammed. I could hear whispers but could make out nothing that was said.

"What are you guys doing?" I asked, my throat tightening.

"Get the blue sweatshirt," Natasha instructed. "Her socks are in there."

No one was answering me. Why was no one answering me? With the blindfold keeping me in pitch-black darkness, I wasn't even sure how many of them were in the room. My palms prickled with heat and it was getting harder to breathe.

Come on, Reed. Play it cool. Don't let them see you sweat.

"This has all been very amusing, you guys, but I'm going back to sleep," I said, reaching for the blindfold again. Another slap. I felt my adrenaline start to rush.

"Stop hitting me!" I snapped.

"Stop *making* me," Kiran shot back.

"Kiran—"

Suddenly my hair was yanked back from my face and I felt hot breath on my ear. I froze. "Shut it, Reed," Noelle said harshly. My heart all but stopped. Her lips were practically touching my ear. She meant business. "This is for your own good."

Someone jammed socks and shoes onto my feet. I tried to suck in some air.

"Now get up."

Two sets of hands yanked me up and turned me around. Someone shoved me from behind and I tripped forward. I had no control and I was terrified. As if at any second I might trip over the stairs or slam into something. As if the whole world might turn upside down. The girls had fallen silent, but I could feel them close in around me. Somehow, that made my heart pound even harder.

As we walked out of my dorm room, I twisted my head from side to side, trying to make the blindfold ride up. Give me a little something, anything, so that when we got out of the dorm I could keep an eye on where we were going. Where were they taking me? Had I, by snapping at Noelle yesterday, broken some cardinal Billings House rule? Even before I got into Billings and Noelle and the others were messing with me every other day, they had never done anything like this. A hundred gory hazing stories gone bad from a hundred evening news broadcasts fizzled through my brain. My temples started to throb.

They wouldn't actually *hurt* me, would they?

For a split second I thought I could see light out of the corner of my eye. But then my coat was thrown over my shoulders and the hood was lifted around my face and everything was dark.

From that moment on, I was at the mercy of the Billings Girls.

LOVE HER

The cold air on my face gave me hope. From what I could tell, we were walking right across the wide-open quad. Someone had to see us. Put a stop to this thing. What time was it? Where were Detective Hauer and his morning stroll when I needed them?

Not that I wanted to get my friends arrested. At least, *part* of me didn't. The other part really wanted to avoid getting my head shaved or being left in the middle of the woods somewhere to find my way home in my pajamas.

"This way. Around here," Noelle whispered.

I was pushed to the right and stumbled slightly, bumping into someone's side. Someone shorter than me and kind of soft. Taylor? Natasha? If they were both still there maybe this would be fine. Natasha was a semi-decent person, and Taylor was too skittish to do anything *really* awful.

I hoped.

Suddenly I was hit with a strong gust of wind and my hood flew off. Light flooded the blindfold and my heart leapt. But I still couldn't see anything. The swirling paisley pattern of blues and greens was just that much brighter. A car engine hummed nearby and I could smell that acrid scent that warming-up engines give off.

A painful knot tied in my stomach. They were taking me off campus.

"You guys, come on," I said, sounding fairly desperate. "What are you—"

"Just get in," Noelle said.

A shove at the small of my back tipped me forward. My hands flew out and touched the side of the car. There was frost on the window. My fingers trembled.

"Get her head," Noelle instructed.

A strong hand pushed my head down and I crawled inside. Vanilla air-freshener choked me. I fell into a seat and immediately reached for the blindfold. Someone sat down beside me, and her hands made it there before mine. My hair was yanked once again as the blindfold was torn free. Tears stung my eyes.

"Surprise!"

There was a pop and a screech and a splatter on my foot. I blinked a dozen times and tried to focus. When I did, I saw that Taylor, Natasha, and Kiran were sitting across from me in the back of a gray limousine, all dressed and fresh-faced and smiling. Natasha handed out champagne glasses while Kiran held a spouting bottle away from her six-hundred-dollar heels.

"What the hell?"

"Reed Brennan, this is your day," Ariana said, reaching for my hand.

Her fingers were cold as ice, but somehow I found them comforting. Perhaps because they were kindly holding mine instead of forcing me to eat cow dung or something. On my other side, Noelle reached out and took three glasses from Taylor. She handed one to me, then grabbed the still-foaming champagne bottle.

"Christov! Let's go!" she shouted. "This hunk of metal isn't going to drive itself!"

"Yes, ma'am," the handsome driver said.

He hit a button over his head and a tinted window slid up, shutting him off from the rest of us. Natasha lifted herself up to mess with a stereo that was set into the ceiling. Two seconds later, party music filled the car. This was definitely a whole new brand of kidnapping.

"Here you go, Reed. Drink up," Noelle said, handing me a full glass.

"Is someone going to tell me what's going on here?" I asked.

"We're taking you for a spa day!" Taylor cried, downing her champagne in one gulp.

"Kiran knows this exclusive place in Boston," Ariana explained, smoothing her slim skirt. "Only models and movie stars are allowed."

"And a few politicians," Kiran said, sipping her drink. "As long as they're dating models or movie stars."

"We got Suzel to pull a few strings and get us all day passes," Noelle said with a smile. "Love her!" she trilled.

"To Suzel!" the girls cheered, clinking glasses and sipping their champagne.

"What's a Suzel?" I asked.

"Suzel. Susan Llewelyn. Board member. Former Billings Girl. Love her," Kiran sang.

"To Suzel!" the girls all cheered again. Another clink. Another sip.

"Suzel thought you deserved a day of distraction," Ariana said. "So this is it."

I found it interesting that Suzel had an opinion on what I might deserve, considering I'd never met the woman.

"Your day," Taylor said with a smile.

"To get your mind off things," Natasha told me, looking me in the eye.

"Exactly! We're here for you, Reed," Noelle said. "Massage, facial, manicure, pedicure. Whatever you need to make you feel relaxed. It's all about you."

I looked at her in her perfect jeans and cozy turtleneck sweater, her thick hair washed and shining and giving off a rich, clean scent. Meanwhile, I smelled like I needed a shower, and I knew I looked ridiculous, my feet sticking out of my pajama pants in my sneakers. I could only imagine what my hair was doing—probably being greasy and knotted and frizzed.

"Really? So what was the kidnapping thing all about?" I asked.

"Oh, that? That was payback," she said, taking a slug from her glass.

"Payback is her favorite pastime!" Kiran said, lifting a glass toward Noelle. Everyone else lifted theirs as well, as if this, too, was something to celebrate. Everyone other than Natasha, who had reasons *not* to rejoice over Noelle's mind games.

"You didn't really think you'd get away with yesterday's little performance without any repercussions, did you?"

Noelle smiled teasingly, and somehow I found myself smiling back. Love her or hate her, this was Noelle. And as I was being whisked off campus in a limousine on my way to a day of beauty at an exclusive spa, I decided to choose "love her."

For now, anyway.

PAMPERED

"London is *not* getting a reduct," Kiran cried, pushing herself out of her cushy chair as her aesthetician finished her facial. She walked over to a slatted-wood counter, where twelve fresh mimosas were lined up, and grabbed one. "That girl lives for those double-D's."

"I'm just telling you what I heard," Taylor replied with a shrug.

"Call me crazy, but I don't believe half the stuff I hear at Easton," Natasha said wryly. A direct commentary on the other girls in the room, I knew.

"I thought you were supposed to be resting quietly," Noelle commented.

Natasha smiled beatifically. She was still lying back in her own chair with a cold blue pillow over her eyes, breathing in and out as instructed. Up until a few minutes ago, Kiran, Natasha, and I had been alone in the small, orange-blossom-scented room with our spa worker bees, but Noelle, Ariana, and Taylor had just rejoined us, having finished their treatments.

"Anyway, Taylor, you're missing an important detail of the story," Noelle said, laying her *W* magazine aside.

Her facial having been finished just a few minutes before, she now sat on the leather couch in the corner with her face covered in purple shellac. Her hair was back in a white towel and her diamond earrings sparkled in her ears. She crossed her legs and her white, waffle-weave robe—standard issue from the spa and exactly like the ones we all wore—fell open to expose her entire thigh.

"London *floated* the rumor that she was getting a reduction so that Vienna would book one over Christmas break," Noelle told us.

"You know how the Twin Cities always need to one-up each other," Ariana put in. She stood against the wall, her arms crossed over her stomach and her legs crossed at the ankle. Her blond hair practically glowed in the soft pink light.

"The idea is that Vienna will come back from break all deflated," Noelle continued. "And London—"

"Will be the only Pam Anderson on campus," Kiran said slowly, narrowing her eyes. "Now that's ingenious."

"Which is exactly why I don't buy it," Natasha said, still blinded. "This is London we're talking about. You know, the girl who asked me if strawberry milk would turn her bones pink?"

"She did not," Ariana said, her jaw dropping.

"Hand to God," Natasha replied, lifting a hand. "The best part being, of course, that I think she *wanted* them to be pink."

Everyone laughed, including me and the girl working on my

face, whose name was Teresa. She shook her head as she finished touching up the area near my temples.

"Your friends are a rare breed," she said with a slight Italian accent.

"Tell me about it," I replied with a smile.

"Okay, you're all done," she told me. "Just relax for twenty minutes and then we'll come give you the final scrub and toner."

"Thank you," I told her, sitting up.

She handed me a glass of cucumber water and slipped from the room. A smile had attached itself to my face without my even thinking about it. My whole body felt so relaxed, it was as if nothing else in the world mattered. Every person on the planet should get a massage and facial every month. It should be an accepted part of normal life, like checkups or haircuts. I could only imagine how much more chill my mother would be if she was able to get pampered every once in a while. Maybe my childhood wouldn't have been all psychodrama all the time. Maybe she wouldn't feel the need to pop all those pills and take out any residual anger on me.

"You look happy," Ariana said, sipping her mimosa.

"I think I am happy," I said.

Noelle and Ariana exchanged an approving, triumphant look. At that moment, one of the cell phones lined up on the bench near the wall trilled. I recognized my ring and jumped down to get it. My heart gave a flutter when I saw Josh's name on the caller ID.

"Who is it?" Ariana asked.

"It's Josh."

I was about to flip the phone open when Noelle grabbed it out of my hand. "No men." She turned the phone off and placed it in the pocket of her robe.

"But I—"

"Eh! This is *our* day," Noelle said, lifting her finger. "No men."

I glanced at her pocket. What was I going to do, tackle her? Not likely. No one wanted to see the repercussions of *that*. Instead, I surrendered. I was not going to argue now. Not when I was feeling this good.

"Josh, huh?" Kiran said. "You two sure have been talking a lot lately."

Everyone was staring at me now, their faces green and purple and white. They were all silent, and for the first time since Noelle and the others had joined us, the soothing bamboo flute music that was being piped in from hidden speakers was actually discernable. I felt the familiar sourness of Thomas-guilt creeping over my shoulders and into my chest, but I refused to let it settle.

"I thought the rule was 'no men,'" I said, walking over to get a drink. "So I suggest we change the subject."

"She's right," Ariana said lightly. "What were we talking about again?"

"What *were* we talking about?" Kiran said, dropping her empty glass and reaching for another. "Oh, yes! Plastic surgery. Would you guys ever do it?"

"Are you kidding? To maintain this?" Noelle said, pointing at her purple face. "Of course. In fact . . ." She looked around conspiratorially as she slid back into one of the facial chairs. "I've already done it."

"You have?" I gasped.

"No! How did I not know this?" Kiran demanded.

"Come on, people. A nose like this does not exist in nature," Noelle said.

I stared at her nose. It *was* darn perfect. But I couldn't believe that Noelle hadn't been born her own, beautiful self. It felt almost wrong somehow, that she was even slightly less blessed that I'd believed.

"I had my chin fixed," Kiran put in. "When I was twelve."

"Your parents let you do that?" Natasha asked, appalled.

"My mother insisted on it," Kiran said with a shrug. "She said I'd never have a career with my wicked-witch chin, so . . . slice!"

She made a cutting motion with her hand under her chin. I cringed. This was very enlightening.

"Oh my God. That is just evil," Taylor said. "Even for your mother."

"Clarissa Hayes has been evil as long as I've known her," Noelle said matter-of-factly.

Kiran stared at a fixed point somewhere on the floor. "Yeah, well, I wouldn't have a billboard in New York if she wasn't."

She swallowed an entire glassful of mimosa in one gulp.

"Has anyone else in Billings had something done?" Natasha asked. I got the idea she was changing the subject for Kiran's sake, rather than because of any real lust for dirt. Aside from the strawberry milk story, I'd never known her to gossip.

"I heard Cheyenne took growth hormones from age ten because the doctors predicted she'd only be four-eleven," Taylor said.

"So obvious," Noelle said. "Check the arms. Have you ever seen her sitting in class? They practically drag on the floor!"

Soon everyone was laughing and gossiping and drinking away any uncomfortableness caused by Josh's call or Kiran's evil mom. I had nothing to contribute, so I sat back in my chair, closed my eyes, and listened to the chatter.

As Natasha and I padded back down the hallway after our manicures and pedicures in our spa-issue slippers, I was perfectly relaxed. My face tingled, my nails were thick with polish, and my feet were softer than pillows. Was this how Kiran and the other girls felt all the time, just walking around on a normal day? Because if so, I could almost understand why they acted so superior. I felt undeniably beautiful.

I wished Thomas could see me. And when I wished it, sorrow seeped into my heart. But it was a softer kind of sorrow than the red-hot anger and confusion I had been feeling for so long. It was a nostalgic, wistful sorrow. A kind that didn't send me hurtling over the edge.

"So, was this a good idea?" Natasha whispered. There was something about the hushed, opulent vibe of this place that made a person want to whisper. "I wasn't sure."

"It was a great idea," I told her. "I almost feel like myself again. Whatever that means."

Natasha's freshly waxed brows came together. "I don't think anyone really knows what that means."

"I don't know if that makes me feel *better* or if it's just really, really sad," I replied. We both smirked. Deep conversations were for another time.

I pushed open the slatted door to the locker area and stopped. Instantly, I recognized the distinct snorts and sniffles of Taylor's sobs. Natasha and I exchanged a look and neither of us moved. A silent agreement. Suddenly I felt all kinds of close to her. We were conspiring together. Me and Natasha. Considering how much conspiring had been done all around and about me since my arrival at Easton, it felt sort of good to be on the other side.

"It's going to be okay," Kiran said in a soothing voice. I'd never heard her sound so gentle. "Taylor, please. Just try to calm down."

Taylor gasped in a breath. "I just . . . I just . . . I just . . . can't—"

"I can't take this anymore," Noelle said. "Taylor, I swear to God, if you don't freaking chill the hell out in the next five seconds, I cannot be held responsible for the shit fit I'm going to throw."

Taylor whimpered, like a hungry dog that had just been kicked by its master. Natasha's and my eyes met. All right, enough was enough. I was "one of them" now, wasn't I? Hadn't they told me that a dozen times? No more secrets and all of that. I had to know what was going on in there.

And saving Taylor from whatever Noelle's "shit fit" would bring seemed like a wise idea.

"Hey, guys!" I said, striding into the small room as if I had just walked in. Natasha, on the ball as ever, fell right in behind me. I looked around at Noelle, Taylor, Ariana, and Kiran, who stood in a square in the center of the room. "Everything okay?"

Taylor turned away from me and ran for the bathroom.

"Where did you come from?" Kiran asked.

"We just got back and I heard Taylor crying," I said. "What's wrong?"

"She's just freaking out because she was rejected from that summer program at Harvard," Noelle said, turning to her locker. "She just called home and found out."

"Getting in would have guaranteed her a spot in their freshman class year after next," Ariana explained. "She so wants to go there," she added, looking pityingly toward the bathroom.

"And on top of everything else that's been happening . . ." Kiran said.

I instantly felt horrible for begrudging Taylor all her tears and mood swings. Somehow I had forgotten that every one of us had other stuff going on. All Taylor's notebooks and folders were stamped with the Harvard University logo. I knew she wanted to go there more than anything and that everyone at Easton, and in her family, expected her to. There was a lot of pressure on her to succeed. Maybe Thomas's death was just screwing with her already raw emotions.

"That sucks," Natasha said. She crossed the room and opened her own locker. "But there has to be someone she could talk to. It's not like we have no connections at Harvard."

Right. Didn't being a Billings Girl guarantee things like this? Automatic acceptance to whatever one wanted acceptance to?

"That's a good point, Natasha," Ariana said, sounding oddly detached. "We should look into that when we get back."

Natasha and I exchanged a look. There was something weird about the way they were all talking. It was too antiseptic. Too clipped.

"And she could still get in next year, right?" I suggested. "It's just not a given."

"Very true," Noelle said calmly, turning away from me to pack her bag. "You should remind her of that when we get in the car."

"Okay," I said. "Maybe I will."

I stepped up next to Natasha to open my locker and she widened her eyes at me and shrugged. *Call me crazy, but I don't believe half the stuff I hear at Easton,* I heard her say in my mind. Words to live by.

PODUNK COPS

Somehow, we were back on campus early that afternoon. I felt like I had been gone for days. Years. That was how different I felt from the angry, tense, scared (I *did* have a blindfold over my eyes) person who had left that morning.

Now I was energized. My skin practically sizzled and my hair felt freakishly soft against my face. Since I hadn't been allowed to shower that morning, Noelle had treated me to a shampoo, deep condition, and blowout before we left—a ridiculously expensive blowout. But worth every penny, especially since I hadn't paid for it.

I pulled some of my wavy brown locks in front of my eyes, just to see how shiny they were. Unbelievable. This could not be my hair.

"Look at her. You'd think no one had ever shampooed the girl before," Noelle said as we made our way around Bradwell.

"What are you gonna do next? Throw your arms out and twirl?" Kiran asked.

I paused, embarrassed. "Actually, I was about to say thank you, but you guys make it so hard. . . ."

"Sorry." Noelle stopped in her tracks and the other girls lined up beside her. "Proceed."

"With what?" I asked.

"The thank you," Noelle replied.

They all looked at me expectantly—even Taylor, with her bloodshot eyes.

"Fine," I said, rolling my eyes slightly just so that they wouldn't think they had me entirely under their thumbs. "Thanks, you guys. Really. I actually feel almost normal. Like, I don't know, like life might actually go on. And I just—"

Suddenly, I realized that Noelle's gaze had wandered past me and over my shoulder. Gradually, all the other girls looked as well. Their expressions changed so abruptly I felt the stone path tilt beneath my feet.

What now?

When I turned around, I saw Dash and Gage stalking toward us with military stiffness. Dash's nostrils were almost as wide as Missy Thurber's, who could have snout-doubled for Seabiscuit. He had a rolled-up newspaper in his hand.

"What happened?" Noelle asked as the boys arrived, blustering and short of breath.

"They let the prick go. They let the freakin' prick go," Dash said.

"They didn't," Ariana said.

Dash shoved the newspaper at Noelle and Ariana, his hands trembling. Slowly, Noelle took the paper in both hands. It was a local publication I had seen around campus before. The headline read MURDER SUSPECT FREED. Beneath it was a picture of a person I assumed to be Rick DeLea walking out of the Easton police station.

"He came up with an alibi," Gage said. "Some crackhead girlfriend, no doubt. We should've known. These podunk cops'll take care of their own over us any day. Even if he is a scum-sucking drug dealer."

Thomas was a scum-sucking drug dealer, too.

I don't know why that was the first thought that came into my head, but it was. And even though it was the truth, I felt guilty for thinking it.

"I don't believe this," Noelle said. "I thought we had this all under control."

"We?" Dash said.

"We. They. You really want to debate pronouns with me right now?" Noelle snapped.

Her skin looked shiny with sweat, and her hand was over her mouth. Seeing her look so thrown was almost more disconcerting than the news itself. Turning in Rick the Townie had been her idea, and clearly, she didn't enjoy being wrong. I glanced at Ariana and Kiran and Taylor. Everyone looked like wide-eyed caricatures of themselves. I wondered if their stomachs felt as tight and empty and sick as mine did. If the police were right, then Thomas's killer was still out there.

"What're we going to do?" I heard myself say.

No one replied. Natasha reached out and slipped her arm around mine, pulling me to her. I had thought this whole thing was over. I had thought the police had done their job.

But now I saw that this was never going to end. That I was going to feel this way *forever*.

How to Go from on Top of the World to Rock Bottom in Less Than Five Seconds: A Cautionary Tale, by Reed Brennan.

SOMEONE ELSE

"He did it. We all know he did. I say we take justice into our own hands," Dash said at dinner that night. His eyes were wide and he was unable to sit still. I had never seen him so fidgety, and every time his hand jerked or he shifted in his seat, I flinched. This guy was primed to blow.

"Does anyone know where this fuckhead lives?" Gage said.

"What are we going for now, mob rule?" Noelle joked.

She seemed to have recovered nicely from her initial shock. Of course, teasing the guys was always good for her mood.

"If that's what it takes." Dash let a bit of spittle fly. "I'm not playing here, Noelle."

Noelle rolled her eyes and sighed. We all stared at one another. It had been like this all through dinner, and neither my stomach nor my nerves were enjoying it.

"Can we talk about something else?" I suggested.

"Maybe he didn't do it," Natasha said.

"What did you say?" Dash blurted.

Noelle leaned back in her chair, shaking her head. Kiran pushed her vegetables around on her plate. Ariana stared down at her book. Taylor was MIA. Probably curled up in a bed in the infirmary, where she seemed to spend half her time lately.

"I'm just saying, clearly they didn't have enough evidence to keep him in custody, so maybe he *didn't* do it," Natasha said, lifting a shoulder. "Sometimes you just have to trust in the system."

"That's good stuff, coming from you," Gage said.

Natasha dropped her fork and crossed her arms on the table. "Is this going to be another 'Republicans are evil' diatribe? Because I *so* don't get enough of those," she said sardonically.

"I'd love to hear about why Republicans are evil," Kiran put in. "At least it would be a change of subject."

"Look, *Gisele*, just because you don't give a shit that Thomas was murdered doesn't mean we shouldn't be trying to figure out who did it," Gage said. "The world does not revolve around Kiran Hayes."

"You think I don't give a shit?" Kiran blurted. Her tone was so venomous, it made me jump. Startled tears came to my eyes and I was instantly embarrassed, but I couldn't control it. I was that on edge. "Who the hell do you think you are? You have no idea what I do and don't care about! I would *love* to know what really happened to Thomas, what the police are thinking. But no one seems to want to tell us, do they? No! They just want us to sit here and suffer."

"Kiran," Ariana said in a warning, soothing tone.

Kiran looked around as if just remembering that anyone other than Gage was at the table. "Sorry. I'm just sick of this," she grumbled. "It's too weird. A few weeks ago he was sitting right there being obnoxious and now we're talking about who did and didn't kill him. I mean—"

"I can't listen to this anymore," I blurted.

I pushed my chair back so hard it slammed into Cheyenne's, who was sitting at the next table. Clumsily, I gathered up my bag and coat. One of the wood buttons whacked Cheyenne on the back of the head and she made a big show of how much it hurt. I ignored her.

"I'll see you guys back at Billings."

"Reed—"

I had already turned to go, but I paused and swung around. "I thought you guys were planning a party for Thomas," I said, looking at Dash and Gage. "Why don't you concentrate on that instead of making everybody even more miserable than they already are?"

I turned and stormed out, narrowing my eyes to try to quell the tears as I shoved through the door and into the cold night. The second I hit the pathway, I slammed directly into Josh.

"Reed! Are you okay?" he asked.

He placed his hands on my arms to steady me. The wind blew a few of his blond curls across his forehead. Being so close to him so suddenly brought on another huge rush of emotion that I wasn't sure I could take. I moved aside and sucked in a broken breath.

"I'm fine," I said, pressing the heel of my hand to my forehead.

Breathe in, breathe out. Remember how you felt this morning. How you felt before everything caved in again. I'm at the spa. I'm cuddled into that soft, soft robe. I'm lying back in the chair, content. . . .

"I was freaking out all day. Where were you?" Josh demanded.

I blinked at him, confused. Ripped from my reverie before I could fully realize it. Was he angry at me for some reason? "I was with Noelle and them."

"Oh." Josh's face became hard as he stood up straight. "I thought we were going to Boston."

I felt as if someone had just dumped a bucket of water over my head. Josh's brother and his girlfriend. The day of fun in Boston. I had completely forgotten about it, what with being forcibly torn from my bed and everything. My heart squeezed as I noticed the depth of disappointment in Josh's face. This had meant a lot to him, and I had completely blown it off. And even as I realized this, I was touched. Josh really wanted to be with me. Introduce me to his brother. Treat me with that level of importance. Which made my forgetfulness that much worse.

"Josh, I am *so* sorry," I said. "I completely forgot. Noelle and Kiran woke me up at the crack of dawn and I was half out of it. I'm an idiot."

"It's fine. Really," he said, all aloof. "It's good to know I'm that forgettable."

He turned to go. Guilt overcame me. All I wanted to do was explain.

"Josh, wait," I said, grabbing his arm.

"No, Reed. It's okay. You'd rather spend the day with your

girlfriends than me. I get it," he snapped. "Message received."

I'd never seen him this angry. Where was this coming from?

"I would not rather spend the day with them than you," I said, desperate. "Believe me."

Josh paused and searched my face. "Yeah?"

"I swear."

Slowly his demeanor relaxed. He rubbed his forehead with his fingertips. "Oh, God. I'm sorry. I was just worried about you. I called you twenty times and I kept getting your voice mail. I was freaking out. I mean, after what happened to Thomas . . ."

I felt like I was trying to swallow my heart. Everything was different now, wasn't it? A few unanswered phone calls and one could reasonably assume disappearance and death.

"Josh, I'm really sorry. I didn't think," I said.

"Why didn't you answer your phone?" he asked. The accusation was gone from his voice, replaced by concern. I took a deep breath, glad to have normal Josh back. He was supposed to be the rock around here.

"Noelle stole my phone," I told him. I shivered in my thin sweater. The hot streak of anger had passed and I suddenly realized I was freezing. I placed my bag on the ground and pulled my coat on. "I really am sorry."

"It's cool," Josh said. "Just . . . next time, don't let her take it. With everything that's been going on . . ."

For a second I thought he was going to reach for my hand, and my heart skipped nervously, but then he thought the better of it.

He shoved his fists into the pockets of his coat instead. My fingers itched for the phantom contact.

"I know," I said. "Won't happen again."

Josh managed a smile. "Good. Because if anything happened to you . . ."

My chest felt warm and full. I had all but forgotten the unpleasantness in the caf.

"Okay," I said. Because there were a million things I wanted to say but couldn't.

Josh leaned back against the brick wall behind him and tipped his head up. He let out a huge sigh.

"So, did you hear about Rick?"

"Yeah," I said. I leaned back next to him. Looked down at my shoes. "It's all anyone can talk about."

"I can't believe it. After all that, they let him go? How incompetent are these people?" he said.

"I know. I feel like we're never going to know what really happened," I said.

"I know what happened," Josh snapped. "Rick and Thomas got into it and Rick killed him. End of story. Why can't these people ever just accept the easy answer?"

I felt something flip in my mind and tried to keep the thoughts at bay, just as I had all day long. But there was no more avoiding it. On they came. If the police were right, if Rick was not the killer, then the killer was obviously still out there. One thing we knew for sure was that Thomas's body had been found in the area. Somewhere near Easton. Rick the townie had made sense because he lived in town, but if it wasn't him, then it stood to reason that it was someone else from around the school. Maybe even someone *at* the school.

Whenever I got to that point on the logic train, my engine died. I just could not wrap my brain around the idea that someone at Easton hated Thomas that much. That someone at Easton was capable of murder.

"I don't know," I said, glancing away.

"It had to be him," Josh said. "It had to be."

"It would make everything so much easier," I said, feeling numb. "Because if it wasn't him, then it was someone else. Maybe someone—"

I couldn't finish the sentence. There was no way.

Josh stared into the darkness. "Maybe someone we know."

A BLIP

"This feels sort of weird," I said as my friends and I approached the Great Room in Mitchell Hall on Tuesday night. I could already hear the dance music pumping through the walls. A few of the former headmasters' portraits were shaking in their gilded frames.

Headmaster Stern from the early 1900s did not look happy about it.

"What doesn't these days?" Natasha asked.

She had a point. Ever since Thomas had died, everything had felt weird. Laughing, eating, talking, studying. But partying, no matter how much we tried to justify it, felt even weirder than everything else.

"All we have to do is get through the next couple of hours," Kiran said with a degree of grimness unfit for a party girl of her caliber. "Then, tomorrow night, we'll all be outta here."

"It will be nice to be home for a few days," Ariana agreed, pausing outside the open double doors. Inside, our classmates milled about, sipping punch and chatting. Some were even dancing. "Get away from all this insanity."

I nodded my agreement, even though I neither a) agreed nor b) was actually going home. On day one, my father had arranged for me to spend Thanksgiving here at Easton with some of the other scholarship students and foreign kids who didn't celebrate the holiday and were too far from home to travel. Getting home was too expensive and just not worth it. Thanksgiving had never been big in the Brennan household anyway—what with so little to give thanks for and a mother whose idea of a big home-cooked meal was ordering in from Boston Market and having it delivered instead of picking it up.

"Shut up, you guys. You're depressing Reed," Noelle said.

"Are you sure you don't want to come home with me?" Natasha asked. She had floated this option earlier in the week, but I had declined. I knew she wanted to spend as much time as possible with Leanne while she was in New York and I didn't want to be in the way. Plus, to be honest, I didn't like Leanne all that much. Or at all. But to each her own.

"Really, I'll be fine," I said, feeling conspicuous. I shook my hair back and smiled, standing up straight. "I heard the apple pie is to die for," I joked.

All the pretty faces around me fell. Everyone looked into the Great Room. My heart thumped. Wow. That had been a highly inappropriate thing to say.

"Let's just go in," I suggested.

"Good plan," Noelle said.

She cleared her throat and led the way. Only a few steps off the plush carpet of the hallway and onto the hardwood floor inside, she stopped. Suddenly I felt as if the whole room was closing in on me.

Thomas was everywhere.

"He has *got* to be kidding me," Noelle said.

Huge photos of Thomas clung to poster board on every available wall surface. Thomas standing in front of Grecian ruins. Thomas two-fisting tropical drinks with a straw hat on his head. Thomas and his brother, Blake, on skis. Thomas on a horse. Thomas with Dash and Gage on the back of some boat named *My Second Bride*. Thomas and Josh in suits and ties. Thomas and some random girl dressed for a formal. Thomas and three big-breasted waitresses. Thomas and an exotic beauty who was licking his face while he grinned.

Thomas. Thomas. Thomas.

And now I couldn't breathe.

Noelle stormed across the room and unleashed that stored-up shit fit on Dash. I turned around to flee.

"Don't."

Ariana's cold hand was on my arm. I felt like all the oxygen was being sucked directly out of my lungs.

"I can't do this. I can't stay here," I said.

Everyone was watching me. Concerned faces. Amused faces. A camera bulb flashed. I felt as if there was a space heater inside my body, emanating heat through my pores. Thomas was dead. Thomas was dead. Thomas was dead.

"Reed, we have to do this. We have to look at him and accept what we've lost," Ariana said. She swallowed, took a breath, and looked around. "We have to accept that he's gone."

My mind felt like it was a whirling moth, trapped inside a lantern, frantically trying to beat its way out. "How can you say 'we'?" I asked. "You don't understand what it's like."

Ariana's eyes were back on me like that. Her lips were thin and white.

"I understand that everyone is watching you," she whispered. Her grip tightened like a claw. "Now, you can either be a weakling who turns and runs, or you can be strong and face this. Your choice."

I knew which one she wanted me to be. Which one even I wanted me to be. The question was whether or not I was up to the challenge.

I turned around slowly and scanned the room. Most of the people who caught my eye quickly looked away. I forced myself to look at the pictures again. Thomas had led such a full life . . . and I had known nothing about it. I had never known he had traveled so much. Never realized that he and his friends were so close. Never known who his family was. Never known how many girls he had been with.

I caught a glimpse of Thomas and his face-licker and was overcome with jealousy and a severe sense of emptiness. Not a single photo had ever been taken of me and Thomas. We hadn't been together long enough, or I hadn't been important enough, for us to be captured on film together.

The moment I thought this, I felt deeply ashamed. How could I stand here feeling sorry for myself? Thomas was dead. He would never have any of these experiences again. All because some psycho out there had felt the need to end his life. God, what I wouldn't give to look that person in the eye and rip his heart out.

"Deep breath," Ariana said. "You can do this."

I inhaled slowly through my nose. *Let Ariana's confidence cool me*. Across the room, Gage smirked in our direction. He and Dash both sported suits and loosened ties and looked very proud of themselves, even as Noelle ranted at them.

"Let's get something to drink," I suggested.

"Now you're talking," Kiran said.

This time, I led the way. When we got to the drink table, I dunked a cup directly into the punch bowl and sucked the fruity liquid down my dry throat. Kiran took a moment to slip out her flask under the table and spike her drink and Taylor's.

"Nice work," I said to Gage. "You guys should go into funeral planning."

"It *is* the only business where you're guaranteed a nonstop flow of customers," Gage replied lightly.

This boy needed a good ass-kicking. Like yesterday. Maybe Noelle should have let them go after Thomas's townie.

"You need to take down the pictures, Dash," Noelle said,

apparently attempting to regain her composure. "It's Tim Burton–level morbid."

"What? I think it's cool," Dash said, admiring his handiwork. "We're supposed to be celebrating Thomas's life. Well, this was his life."

"It's creepy," Kiran said, shuddering as she took a sip of her punch. "It's like he's staring at us."

"From beyond the grave," Taylor put in.

Gage scoffed. "And the Oscar for superfluous drama goes to—"

Dash laughed and the two boys slapped hands. "Nice!"

"This from the guys who were forming a lynch mob just days ago," Noelle said, rolling her eyes.

"I don't understand you, Noelle. Did I or did I not ask for your help planning this, and did you or did you not turn me down cold?" Dash asked, squaring his broad shoulders.

Noelle's eyes narrowed. I felt a lovers' spat coming on. "What's your point?"

"My point is, you didn't want to get involved, so now you don't get to complain about it," he said.

Noelle's mouth fell open. Dash looked mighty proud of himself. No one, not even Dash McCafferty, rendered Noelle speechless very often. Could it be that the balance of power in this relationship was shifting? You could practically see the hope in his eyes.

"Why don't you girls all down some of Kiran's secret stash and unclench?" Gage said, with his usual subtlety. "Meanwhile, we'll be over here letting Dean Marcus congratulate us on a job well done."

Gage slapped his hand down on Dash's shoulder and tugged him away. Noelle fumed silently as she watched the guys lope casually across the room. She wasn't big on making scenes, but I knew Dash was going to pay for that one later. Possibly, she was already plotting her revenge.

"I'm sorry about this, Reed," she said. "I suppose etiquette and testosterone cancel each other out."

I took a sip of my punch and set the glass down on the table. "You don't have to apologize for them, Noelle," I said. "It's good, actually. Ariana's right. I need to face this head-on. I need to stare right into the face of the guy who said he loved me and then lied to me and was then brutally murdered. In fact, I think it'll make the whole mourning-process thing that much easier."

"Reed—"

I was ranting. Billings Girls didn't rant.

"I'm going to the bathroom now," I told Ariana. "Or does that make me a weakling too?"

She opened her mouth to speak.

"Actually, forget it. I don't care," I said, cutting her off. "I'm going now, and when I get back, I'm going to dance."

"I'll be ready!" Kiran said, raising her glass.

My eyes were dry as sand as I wove my way back through the room. Reality was finally setting in on me. Thomas was gone. And even when he had been here, I had been just a blip to him, a nothing.

A nothing who seriously had to move on.

PLEASANT DEVELOPMENT

"Are you all right? You look like you're evaporating," Josh said, handing me a glass of iced punch.

I was taking a break from my cathartic dance ritual and my skin was beaded with sweat, but it felt good. It felt like I was getting something out of my system. I just hoped whatever it was didn't smell.

I took a sip of the fruity punch and watched Noelle, Kiran, and Taylor, who apparently still had stuff to work out. They were all out there, hogging the center of the dance floor. I saw a few non-Billings girls shooting them snide looks behind their backs, but whenever one of my friends turned their eyes on the same girls, they were all smiles. Such power.

"I'm fine," I said casually. "What do *you* think of the decorations?"

Josh looked around. "I'm gonna go with cool but eerie."

I smirked. "Where's that one from?" I asked, lifting my hand toward the shot of him and Thomas all dressed up. I tried to look at Josh instead of Thomas. Pretend Thomas wasn't there. Pretend I was just a-okay, hunky-dory, peachy-keen. All phrases my fourth-grade teacher, Mrs. Cornerstone, had used on a daily basis.

"That was Penny Halston's wedding the week before school started," Josh replied. "The guy she married has some stake in the Anheuser-Busch Companies, so they had bottled beer at the reception. Thomas snagged, like, a whole dolly full of cases and stayed up all night drinking, just to see how far he could get."

I shook my head and looked at the floor. Were there any Thomas stories that didn't include him being wasted?

"When we found him at dawn, he was lying on the eighteenth green, singing 'Ninety-nine Bottles of Beer' and flinging the empties into a sand trap," Gage said with a laugh, joining us.

"Almost killed one of the landscaping crew," Josh added.

"Whatever. Like twenty stitches is such a big freaking deal." Gage took a slug of his drink. "Kid did know how to party, though. But you knew that, didn't you, Brennan?" he asked lasciviously.

He reached out as if to run his finger down my arm. Josh shoved Gage's shoulder about two seconds before I would have grabbed Gage's finger and twisted. "You have serious problems, you know that?" Josh spat.

"Look who's talking, Hollis," Gage shot back.

Josh glanced at me as if snagged. *Huh?*

"Back off, asshole," he said to Gage.

The last thing I needed right now was a scene. "Guys, come on—"

"Oooh. I'm so scared." Gage set his drink down. "You think I'm scared of you, freak? Let's go."

"At least I'm not pathological," Josh retorted.

"Well, maybe it just hasn't been diagnosed!"

Another shove. Even trash-talking was more sophisticated at Easton. Bigger words, subtler insults.

"Whoa, whoa, whoa!" Dash walked over with his hands raised and lowered them onto Gage and Josh's shoulders, with me in between. The man had a serious wingspan. "This is supposed to be a party. Everyone mellow out."

"Mellow out? What have you been smoking?" Gage said, still belligerent.

"Nothing. I'm just saying, what's there to fight about? All our friends are here, we've paid our tribute to Pearson, and day after tomorrow we'll be home gorging on the best food of the year," Dash said, leaning back against the wall next to Gage. "It's all good."

"Speak for yourself, dude," Gage said. He took a step back from Josh. "Somehow I don't think my mom's new Venezuelan cook is going to know how to work a turkey."

Subject officially changed. Josh's shoulders uncoiled and Gage seemed to have already forgotten he was about to tear someone's head off. Dash was *good*. Not for the first time, I appreciated his maturity and levelheadedness. He never stooped to join in with Gage's random mockery and insults and was always able to defuse awkward situations. Plus, he'd managed to be in a solid relationship with Noelle for three years—an achievement in and of itself. I saw politics in his future.

"Thank you," I mouthed to Dash. The last thing I could handle just then was a pummeling between supposed friends. I'd already had enough drama for one semester. Dash nodded in response. I looked out at the dance floor and waited for my heartbeat to return to normal.

"Has your mother *ever* hired an American?" Dash asked Gage.

"Mara Coolidge? Champion of the should-never-be-employed? No," Gage said.

"Well, I will be eating a nice home-cooked meal at my grandmother's manse," Dash said, glassy-eyed at the prospect. "Turkey, cranberries, stuffing, the whole nine."

"Oh, you are so the all-American boy," Gage said, reaching out to pinch Dash's cheek. "What about you, new girl?" Gage asked. He walked over to the nearest table and sat, legs spread. We all followed, Dash and me sitting between Josh and Gage, just in case of a relapse. "What's turkey day like in Bumblefuck, Pennsylvania? Turkey roll and Bud from a can?"

Love this guy. *Love* him.

"Dude, back off," Josh snapped.

"Josh," I said. Like, *Calm down already.* I appreciated the effort, but I could take care of myself. "Actually, I'm not going home," I told them. "I'm staying here."

"You are?" Josh asked. His eyebrows shot up under his curls. "So am I."

Really? This was an unexpected and pleasant development. A warm sensation prickled over my skin. I was actually going to have a friend here. Someone to eat with. Someone to talk to. And not just someone, but Josh. The two of us. Here alone. With no one to watch us or judge and comment. Suddenly, the long four-day weekend was looking *much* better.

"What?" Dash and Gage blurted at once. "Come on, man. The Hollis Thanksgivings are legendary," Dash added.

Josh tore his eyes away from mine and cleared his throat. I hid a smile by suddenly becoming very interested in the dance floor and fluffing my hair alongside my face.

"Not this year," Josh said, leaning into the table to better see Gage and Dash. "My parents are stuck in Germany so the kids are going to my aunt's house on the Cape and Lynn's gonna be with his girl. Neither one appealed, so—"

"So you'd rather stay here," Gage said incredulously. "Alone."

Under the table, Josh's fingers grazed mine. My heart spasmed and I turned my hand palm up on my thigh. Josh took it, cupping my fingers with his. The flush started at my wrist and shot straight up my arm and throughout my body. I tried my hardest not to smile.

"Yeah," he said with a smirk, squeezing my hand. "Alone."

OUT OF CHARACTER

The party, inevitably, got out of control. It was clear to the world that Kiran had not been the only "mourner" to smuggle in alcohol. All that was left to be determined was when the dean's gradually simmering anger would finally go nuclear, putting an end to the evening, and whether or not there would be any repercussions. On the dance floor, Kiran, London, and Vienna twirled and whirled, falling all over one another and laughing their toned butts off. Dash was dancing with himself. Missy Thurber stepped slowly back and forth, clinging to one of the guys from my history class—even though the song playing was an upbeat one—half-asleep and drooling on his shoulder. He looked down the back of her dress, undoubtedly trying to determine whether or not he could manage to unhook her bra without her noticing. Considering her present state, I gave him two-to-one odds.

Over in the far corner, Walt Whittaker and Constance Talbot were talking with their heads bent close together. They had been there most of the night. Every once in a while Constance would smile and blush and Whit would preen, pleased with himself. Looked like Constance had finally bagged her lifelong crush. Good for her.

"Dean Marcus has checked his watch ten times in the last three minutes," Natasha pointed out. "What's he waiting for?"

"He's probably hoping we all survive until ten o'clock without anyone making a scene or passing out," Ariana replied. "He did tell Dash we could have the room until then. This way he won't have to go back on his word."

"Always toeing the line, that Marcus. I bet he was a real wild man as a kid," Josh joked.

Natasha and I laughed and Ariana smiled. We were all sitting at one of the round tables, people-watching. I felt exhausted and almost content after a night of dancing, chatting, and laughing. I barely even noticed the photos of Thomas anymore, and when I did, I refused to let them bother me. From now on, nothing Thomas-related was going to bother me.

"What the hell!?"

My eyes shot to the door. Someone was shouting. A few people ran over to see what was going on. My heart drooped. What *now*? There had been so much drama lately, they should be turning Easton into a theater-in-the-round. Someone was freaking out, but their words were unintelligible over the music. Ms. Ling, the cutesy Bradwell housemother, and Mr. Shreeber, the cross-country coach and Spanish teacher, raced over to see what was going on. Soon most of the kids in the room were moving toward the door, jostling for a better view.

"What are you thinking?! Do you have no self-control?!"

My heart seized. I knew that voice.

"That's Noelle," Natasha said.

Ariana was already on her feet.

"That's it. I can't even look at you anymore!" Noelle shouted, storming back into the room with Ms. Ling on her heels. Noelle's face was blotchy with rage. She looked over her shoulder at Taylor, who was pale and unsteady on her feet. "I swear to God, sometimes I don't even know why we let you in."

There was an audible gasp from somewhere in the crowd. A Billings Girl questioning the worth of another Billings Girl was heresy to the commoners. When alone with each other, of course, we did it all the time. But it was never done in public.

"Noelle," Ariana gasped. Though there was no way Noelle could have heard her from halfway across the room.

Dash stepped forward and tried to take Noelle's hand, but she snatched her arm away. She grabbed her clutch, then turned and walked out the emergency-exit door into the night. After the briefest hesitation, Ariana followed her. I had never seen her look so stunned. For a long moment, no one moved. My heart pounded so hard it hurt. Something must really have pissed off Noelle for her to have gone that ballistic in public.

Ms. Ling slipped her arm around Taylor's shoulders and helped her back out into the hallway. Two seconds after they were gone, Gage slid into the Great Room through the same door, hands in his pockets, looking amused and sheepish all at once. He might as well have been casually whistling.

Dash made a beeline for Gage.

"Let's go," Natasha said, grabbing my hand.

She, Josh, and I followed Dash into the corner with Gage. Kiran was already there.

"What the hell just happened?" Dash asked Gage.

Behind us, the music stopped and the dean announced that the party was over. A bunch of people groaned. We ignored him.

"Nothing, dude. I swear," Gage said.

"Well, something obviously happened," Natasha said.

Gage narrowed his eyes. "I don't know, all right? I'm coming back from hitting the head and I see Taylor sitting on the floor in the hallway all weepy. So I ask her if she's okay, right? I'm a gentleman."

He pulled down on his cuffs. Kiran, Natasha, and I all scoffed. Dash shot us a silencing glare.

"So she says no, she's not okay, and she's all snotty and everything, so I sit down next to her and ask her what's wrong," Gage continued.

"Why?" Natasha asked, voicing the thought on everyone's mind. Gage was not known for his compassion.

"Because he figured he could get some," Josh said under his breath.

"Whatever, dude. She's not even my type," Gage shot back.

"Gage, what happened with Noelle?" Dash asked through his teeth.

"That's just it, man. I have no idea. Taylor's blubbering all over me, making no sense. She's saying all this crap about Thomas and how sad it is and how his parents will never know what happened to him now, and all of a sudden, Noelle comes storming out and goes all Emily Rose all over the place. I swear to God, it was like she was possessed. She practically ripped the girl off the floor just so she could get in her face."

Dash looked completely confused. Much like I felt.

"I have to go talk to Taylor," Kiran said, turning to go.

"I'll come," I offered.

"No!" Kiran snapped. I flinched and she paused and took a deep breath. "Sorry. It's just, I know her better than you do. I think I'd better go alone."

Then she hightailed it out of there before I could even find the words to protest.

LONELY TRAVELER

I awoke with a start, my heart racing so quickly I might have just run a mile. I was half asleep, but I had the distinct impression I had just heard a door slam. My room was one notch lighter than black. The digital clock read 5:32 a.m. Natasha was asleep on her back, her mouth hanging open. Had I dreamt it?

A bang sounded in the hall and I sat up straight. I tried to quiet my own breath and listened. Someone was moving past my door. I heard the distinct creaking of the ancient Billings House stairs. Moments later, the front door of the dorm opened, then slammed.

I quietly slipped out of bed and tiptoed over to the window by my desk. The campus grounds were covered with a thick, wet fog, and the old-fashioned torch lamps that dotted the pathways gave off a pathetic, fuzzy glow. Down below, the grayness swirled. Someone was walking along the path. Whoever it was wore a black hat and pulled a huge suitcase on wheels behind her—huge enough for a monthlong trip. Just when I thought I'd never get a good enough look at the lonely traveler, she stepped under one of the old-fashioned street lamps. I recognized Taylor's blond curls.

My already racing pulse started to sprint. Where was Taylor going? It was too early to leave for break. We still had a whole day of classes. Taylor did not miss class.

Dammit. Taylor couldn't go. Not this way. Not before anyone cleared up what had happened last night, what was going on between her and Noelle. Not before I figured out what the hell was happening with her.

As quietly as possible, I unlatched the window lock and slid the pane open a few inches. I had no idea what I was hoping to hear, but I didn't want to miss anything that might clue me in to what was going on. Cold air rushed into the room and I clenched my teeth to keep from shivering. I could hear the wheels of Taylor's suitcase bumping along the stone path. Then something else moved down below. My heart caught in my throat. Someone was following Taylor.

I almost shouted a warning, but in the next second I choked it back. Suddenly I recognized the trench coat, the wide shoulders. They belonged to Detective Hauer.

Why would the police be trailing Taylor? Had Hauer just been out for his morning stroll early today and happened to see her?

Taylor disappeared around Bradwell. Hauer followed. Moments later I heard the pop of a car door closing. Lights flashed against the wall of fog. A sleek black town car swung into view between Bradwell and Dayton, then slipped down the hill toward the Easton gates.

I stood there and waited for Hauer to reappear, but he never did. He had gone off in another direction, or he was hiding out somewhere . . . or he had gotten in the car with Taylor. But why? What was going on?

I sat down on the edge of my bed, feeling suddenly overcome. There I sat and listened until the sounds of the car engine faded into the fog and the car officially vanished, taking Taylor and about a hundred unanswered questions with it.

There was no going back to sleep. I tried to do work until everyone else started to wake up and start the morning ritual of blow-drying, plucking, and garment-swapping, but I just ended up staring at the wall.

All through breakfast I waited for someone to mention Taylor's absence. No one said a word. The talk was all who was leaving when and who was going to shop where and how the NYC people were all going to meet up over the weekend. Was it just me, or was Noelle's nonchalance a little more studied this morning?

I had to bite my tongue to keep from asking. I don't know why, exactly, but I didn't want to be the one to bring it up. It was almost like a game. How long could they continue acting as if nothing was wrong? How long could we all keep up the charade?

A long time, apparently, because soon I found myself sliding into a pew at morning services and still, no one had so much as mentioned the T word. What was up with this school? It was like keeping secrets was everyone's favorite pastime—when they weren't busy gossiping. The whole place was a functioning contradiction.

"Omigod. What is up with Taylor Bell?"

My heart skipped a beat. I looked at Constance's eager face. Trust my former roommate always to play forward for Team Gossip. Considering I was constantly surrounded by the starting lineup of the Secret-Keepers, Constance was good to have around.

"What do you mean?"

Constance settled in next to me and nestled her backpack under her feet. "Kiki totally saw her getting into a car on the circle this morning *way* before the sun even came up."

"What? How?" I asked.

"Girl never sleeps. She's the queen of insomnia. Maybe that's why she won firsts. Nothing else to do in the middle of the night but study," Constance said. She pondered this for a moment, maybe wondering if *she* could become an insomniac and thereby become celebrity for a day, then got back to the subject at hand. "But anyway, she saw the license plate on the car and guess what it was?" she asked, lowering her voice.

I was about three seconds from imploding. "What?"

"It was Hayes three," Constance said. "It was one of Kiran Hayes's mother's cars, but Kiran wasn't with her! What's up with that?"

Suddenly I had that awful sour feeling—that feeling that comes over you when you first realize that everyone around you knows more than you do. That you're completely idiotic and stupid and have missed something completely. I turned around in my pew to look at Kiran, who sat a few rows back with the juniors. She sat straight, with her eyes focused on the front of the chapel. There was an empty space next to her, a space that the other girls in the junior class had left open for Taylor, who was always at Kiran's side. Little did they know that Taylor would not be present this morning.

But Kiran knew. Kiran knew a lot more than she was letting on. I stared at her, willing her to look at me, but she refused, even though I could *tell* she knew I was staring.

Dean Marcus stepped to the podium to begin the service. I faced forward again, so angry I was practically shaking. No more secrets, huh? And I had believed it. Someone should really have tried selling me a bridge already. I was the easiest mark ever.

LAST DITCH

From the high-backed chair near the front window of Billings, I was able to keep watch on both the main door *and* the stairs. Kiran had been avoiding me all day, but I was not going to let her leave campus without talking to me. I had to know what was going on. A cozy fire crackled in the fireplace in our lobby, and Rose and Vienna sat in front of it, chatting, surrounded by at least a half dozen pieces of luggage as they waited for their rides. I just hoped their being there didn't get in the way of my mission.

From my vantage point I was able to see all of my housemates on their way out for the holiday. A couple of parents picked up their daughters, but there were more drivers than family members. Something about the whole procedure made me feel sad and empty, even though it hardly seemed to faze any of the girls. They were used to it, I supposed. And hell, I was the one who wasn't even invited home for Thanksgiving, so who was I to judge?

One of the drivers I had seen come in, a tall, handsome guy with a layer of peach fuzz on his head and a tiny, triangular bit of hair under his bottom lip, appeared at the top of the stairs. I recognized the Louis Vuitton luggage under his arms and stood up. Kiran appeared, wearing a sleek red dress, black boots, a fur-collared coat, and red lipstick. She took one look at me and blew out a sigh.

"I don't have time right now, Reed," she said, slipping on her dark sunglasses as she descended the stairs behind her driver. "Call me over the weekend. You have my cell number, right?"

"No way. You've been avoiding me and I want to know why," I told her under my breath. I glanced at Rose and Vienna. They appeared interested but confused. I could tell that the crackle and pop of the fire were masking our conversation.

Kiran scoffed. "I have not been avoiding you. I've been busy packing. Get over yourself."

"Where's Taylor, Kiran?" I asked.

"She went home," Kiran said flatly.

"Yeah, in one of your cars," I said.

Kiran paused. The driver was halfway out the front door, but he turned to look at her. "Problem, Miss Hayes?"

Kiran shook her head. "No, no. I'm fine. I'll be right behind you."

He shot me a suspicious look that made me think he was more of a bodyguard than a driver, then shoved his way through the door. Kiran pushed her sunglasses to the top of her head and looked at me in an almost pitying way.

"Why did no one even mention that she slunk off in the middle of the night?" I demanded. "Why did she take one of your cars?"

Kiran glanced at our audience, then pulled me into the alcove behind the front door and practically shoved me against the wall. "Will you shut up?" she said through her teeth. She glanced back into the house, then very deliberately straightened her back, rolled her shoulders, and looked down her nose at me. "How did you find out about that?"

"One of my friends saw her leave," I said, my pulse racing. "Kiran, what is going on?"

Kiran scratched just above her eyebrow and breathed in. She lifted her head, and when she looked at me again, she was all smiles.

"What's going on is you're paranoid," Kiran said. "No one mentioned Taylor *slinking* out of here because she did not slink. The only flight she could get back to Indiana was early this morning, so I offered to have one of my mother's drivers come up and take her. We all *knew* she was leaving early."

"I didn't," I said.

"Well, forgive us if this incredibly pertinent bit of information didn't trickle down," Kiran said sarcastically. "There's been kind of a lot going on lately. Now if you'll excuse me, I don't like to keep Helmut waiting."

"Hang on," I said, stopping her before she could make it to the door. "If you all knew about it, then why did you just freak when you found out I knew about the car?"

Kiran turned to look at me, impatient. "What?"

"You just slingshotted me in here when I said something about the car. Like you didn't want anyone to hear me. If everyone knew she was leaving early, then what's with all the cloak and dagger?" I asked.

"Well, Reed, it's not like I want it advertised that I'm just giving people free rides everywhere," Kiran said smoothly. "Word gets out and everyone in this dorm is going to be all over me for trips to Boston and rides to the airport. Like I really need that kind of stress in my life."

I stared at her. She was good, but I didn't believe her. She knew I didn't believe her. And that's why, two seconds later, without so much as a goodbye, she slammed the door in my face.

To: taylor_bell@gmail.com
From: rbrennan391@aol.com
Subject: Are you okay???

Hi Taylor,

I'm writing because you're not picking up your cell and I don't have your home number. I wanted to talk to you last night after your fight with Noelle, but Kiran told me to wait. You seemed really upset and then I didn't get to see you this morning, so I just wanted to make sure you're okay.

Anyway, I saw you leave early this morning and . . . I don't know. I just felt weird about it. Kiran says I'm just being paranoid, but I feel like something's really wrong. I can't help it. I'm worried. So write back if you get a chance and tell me I'm insane.

I hope you're okay.

Love,
Reed

THANKSGIVING

That night I checked my e-mail on Natasha's computer about once every five minutes, but Taylor never wrote back. I hoped she was just busy with family stuff and that she wasn't avoiding me too. If she decided to avoid me, then I might never find out what was really going on around this place. That was not an option.

With everyone gone, having fled Easton for the airport or for the posh neighborhoods of various eastern-seaboard cities, Billings House felt eerie and still. No shouts and giggles, no music blaring, no fevered study sessions. It was a completely different place. I walked the carpeted halls, for the first time closely studying the photographs of former Billings Girls—until I started to feel as if their ghosts were watching me. Then, irrationally spooked, I went around and opened all the doors to all the bedrooms until the Billings housemother, Mrs. Lattimer, tracked me down and told me to kindly quit making so much noise. I finally retreated back to my room.

After a little while, I started to relax. Yes, the place was silent as a grave, but that also meant that there was no one around to walk into my room and demand something of me. No one to remind me of tragedy. Maybe alone was good. Finally, I settled in to catch up on my reading and actually got some work done. Every time thoughts of Thomas tried to invade, I just concentrated harder on taking notes. I ended up falling asleep with a book open on my lap and didn't turn out the light until my notebook hit the floor and scared me half to death.

On Thursday I slept late, called my brother to wish him luck at the homestead (he was in for the Boston Market feast, though I had no idea why), and talked to my dad as well—making sure he knew that I was perfectly fine and that no one else had gone missing from school. My mother took the phone for three minutes to give me a nonstop diatribe about how it wasn't safe at Easton and I should come home. Not because she was worried about me, but because she didn't want me to have anything I actually wanted. Then my father got back on to talk about my report card and wonder if straight B's and one A were enough to maintain my scholarship (which, by the way, they were). I couldn't get off the line fast enough.

Some time after noon I took a long run around the campus, taking in the deserted walkways and darkened windows. There wasn't a soul in sight. I took the time to admire the beauty that was Easton. Even with bare trees and flowerless beds, the campus was far more elegant than any block of land back home. Every inch of every building evoked tradition and pride, from the beautiful stained-glass windows set deep within the stone walls of the chapel to the columns marking the entrance to Easton Library. There was no trace of the modern world here. And without all the Bluetooth phones and PSPs and iPods around, I could almost imagine what it had been like to stroll these paths back when the school was founded. All tweed suits and school ties and leather-bound books. Back when things were simple. The longer I jogged, the more solitary I felt. I might as well have owned the place.

Apparently, even Detective Hauer had gotten Thanksgiving Day off. I kept expecting to see him lurking like I had the morning before, but he was nowhere to be found. I started to wonder if I'd imagined his presence in the fog the previous morning. Maybe I had been half-dreaming. Maybe it hadn't happened at all. And if it hadn't happened, I should stop obsessing about it.

For now, that was a tack I was willing to take.

That afternoon I checked my e-mail again. Still nothing. I shot off another missive to Taylor, telling her she didn't have to talk about anything she might not want to talk about. Telling her I just wanted to know that she was all right. Then I turned off the computer and promised myself I wouldn't check again until the next day.

By the time I arrived at the cafeteria that night for the scheduled seven o'clock holiday meal, I felt rejuvenated. I was going to sit down, have a nice dinner, and not think about Thomas, Taylor, Hauer, Rick the townie, or anyone else.

Anyone other than Josh, who was already seated at the end of a table in the center of the room. He wore a corduroy jacket over a blue shirt and looked so handsome I felt unworthy. Candles flickered along the length of the table and cornucopia centerpieces sat on beds of autumn leaves. There were a total of three tables set this way, all in the middle of the room. At the first sat Mrs. Lattimer, with a few other faculty members. At the second was a klatch of foreign students. Josh sat at the third, with a few other scholarship students at the far end, their noses buried in books as they ignored one another.

The place smelled amazing. Roasting turkey, gravy, freshly baked bread. I glanced behind me at the buffet line, but it was empty.

"What's going on?" I asked Josh.

I folded the skirt I had "borrowed" from Kiran's Closet of Dreams under me and sat. God bless the person who had opted not to put locks on our doors. Kiran didn't want to tell me the truth? Fine. Then for the next three days, her stuff was my stuff.

"Table service," Josh said. "Guess that's what happens when only twenty people are eating."

"Wow. It's like we're royalty."

Josh leaned across the table and glanced at the next one over. "Actually, I think one of those guys *is* royalty."

I laughed just as the kitchen doors opened, spilling forth a half dozen cafeteria workers and their trays. Soon platters of sliced turkey, bowls of potatoes, stuffing, and vegetables, and baskets of rolls were laid out in front of us. Already I could tell this was going to be the best Thanksgiving dinner of my life.

"Once you're finished, we bring out the dessert," our server told us with a slight dip of the head. "Apple pie and ice cream."

"Thanks," I replied.

She was already on her way back to the kitchen, but she paused and smiled back at me, as though no one had ever said thanks to her before.

"Ready to feast?" Josh asked.

He was already holding a few slices of turkey over my plate with a huge fork.

"Bird me," I said.

Josh grinned and weighed our plates down with tons of food. Once he had everything he wanted, he dumped a ladleful of gravy over all of it, even the roll. He watched me as I covered only the meat in gravy.

"Wuss," he said.

"I just like it the way I like it."

"So, what're you doing later?" Josh asked. "I don't know about you, but I was bored off my ass today."

"What did you do?" I asked.

"Painted a little. Called my parents. Called my brother. Called my aunt's house and defused an argument between Tess and Tori having to do with sleeping arrangements," he said. "They're twins. Thirteen-year-old female twins with opposite personalities. It's no fun."

"What was the argument?" I asked.

"My aunt put them in the bunk room, as always," he said.

"They were fighting over who got to sleep in the bottom bunk. Three years ago they were fighting over who got to sleep in the *top* bunk. I don't get girls."

"We are a mysterious people," I said.

Josh laughed, his eyes shining in the candlelight.

"You must be a really good big brother," I said. "Most guys wouldn't bother trying."

"Just hoping to save the world from nuclear meltdown," Josh said. "Do you have any siblings?"

"Just my brother, Scott," I said. "He's older."

"What's he like?"

"I have no complaints," I answered.

"And where's he this weekend?"

"Home with the parents," I said. "Actually, if I were looking out for him, I'd be there too. Although he's better off there alone than I would be."

"Volatile situation?" Josh asked.

I froze. How had I let a detail like that slip? I never talked to anyone about my home life. Except Thomas.

"Nothing out of the ordinary," I said, then filled my mouth with potatoes.

Josh watched me for a moment, and I had a feeling he was going to ask me something, but instead he changed the subject.

"So, do you want to hang out after this?" he asked.

I glanced around to see if anyone at the faculty table had heard him. They were all too involved in their meals and their hushed conversation.

"I don't know. How would we get past Lattimer?" I asked.

"She does have certain hawklike qualities," Josh said, looking over at her. My dorm mother was cutting her food into tiny morsels and lifting them to her pinched lips with clipped, precise movements. "We can go to my dorm."

"Please. Mr. Cross will totally hear us," I said. "You're the only one in the entire building. He's got nothing to distract him."

"Reed, look at the man. He's about four hundred years old. If he gets enough turkey in him, he'll pass out before he even gets to Ketlar."

I glanced over my shoulder. Mr. Cross lifted a napkin to wipe gravy from his moustache. Then he took a second helping of turkey. Seconds already.

"Looks like we're good to go, then," I said with a smile.

Josh smiled back. "Looks like."

A SOFT PILLOW

"So, wait. You've never broken a bone? Not one?" Josh asked in awe as we approached Ketlar. "How is that possible?"

The air was crisp and cold, and ten thousand stars winked at us from above. I tipped my head back and turned around, feeling heady and drunk, even though there wasn't an ounce of alcohol in my system. I was practically tingling from the novelty of the evening—the campus so deserted and still, the amazing food, laughing nonstop with Josh through dinner with no one watching me. Plus there was the anticipation of what might be to come. Maybe nothing. Maybe something. I didn't want to think about it too hard. That always seemed to ruin things.

"Perfect balance, stunning athleticism, fear of hospitals," I replied. "Why? Have you?"

I put my arms out and turned in a circle, enjoying the feeling of my hair down my back, the feeling of freedom I was experiencing. Savoring every minute of it.

"Are you kidding? I was a menace as a kid. Falling out of trees, falling off of bikes, falling down stairs. If it was in my sight, I fell off of it. You should have seen the time I broke my pinky. The bone was completely sticking out the side of my hand. My brother even threw up. It was totally wicked," he rambled nervously. He shoved his hands into his coat pockets and shivered, bouncing a little on his toes.

I bit my lip to keep from grinning too hard. I was making him nervous. Clearly, he wanted something to happen here. His manic behavior was giving it all away.

"I even broke my jaw!" he announced, like it was an achievement.

"Really? How?"

"That's what happens when parents drag their kids to country houses where there's nothing to do," Josh told me. "It was in Litchfield. Lynn and I were bored, so we tried to break the sound barrier on my Razor scooter. There was a brick missing in the sidewalk and I went airborne. A bike rack broke my fall. Excruciating. Excruciating! Plus I had to have my mouth wired shut for, like, ever."

I cracked up laughing, stopped twirling, and fell sideways into Josh, nearly knocking us both over.

"Oh, yeah. You have perfect balance," Josh said, laughing as well.

For some reason this made me double over and gasp for breath. I felt like Josh was somehow feeding me laughing gas. No guy had ever had that effect on me before.

"Get it together, Brennan. We're supposed to be stealth here," he teased.

"You're the one who hasn't shut up since we left dinner," I pointed out.

He stared at me for a second, his eyes searching mine, back and forth, back and forth, like they couldn't figure out what to focus on. "Right. You're right. Sorry. I'll stop now."

"No. It's okay," I said, laying a hand on his arm. "Let's just both whisper from here on out."

"Good plan. Good plan," Josh said.

He reached for the door and held his finger to his lips, widening his eyes comically. I nodded and tried not to laugh. Together we slipped inside and Josh held the heavy door until it closed, making sure the click was minimal. Inside, he pointed at Mr. Cross's door and once again widened his eyes in warning. Ever so quickly, we tip-toed past the closed door. The second we were in front of it, a giggle welled up in the back of my throat. I slapped my hand over my mouth. What was wrong with me? Did sneaking around really make me this giddy? Doing it with the Billings Girls had never had this effect.

Of course, none of them was as cute as Josh, nor did they smell as good.

I snorted.

"What are you doing?" Josh whispered.

Then he grabbed my hand and ran.

Covering the ten yards to the end of the hall felt like it took ten minutes. Mr. Cross was going to walk out of his room any second.

We were doomed. My heart was in my throat, but I was smiling. This was fun. Actual fun. And then we were safely behind the door.

"Sorry. Sorry," I said, out of breath. "I just couldn't help it."

"You're dangerous to have around, you know that?" Josh said, his chest heaving. He glanced over his shoulder at the door, as if he could see through the heavy wood.

"Do you think he heard us?" I asked, stepping closer to him.

"No. No. He's probably snoring already," Josh said.

He turned his face back to me and our noses touched. There was a split second of hesitation. A distinct sizzle of warmth in the air. I could practically hear his heart pounding through his shirt. My hand reached up and gently touched his chest. He stared at it as if wondering why it was there.

And then he grabbed me. He grabbed both my arms in his hands and kissed me. Hard. So hard I stumbled backward against the wall. We broke contact for a split second, but then he was on me again, kissing me like his life depended on it. Mashing my lips against his own. I couldn't even begin to try to kiss him back. It was all wrong. All completely and totally wrong.

Thomas had never kissed me like this. Thomas had made me feel special and beautiful and cared for every time we kissed. Thomas . . .

A sob welled up in my throat. I couldn't breathe. I reached up and shoved Josh away from me.

"What happened?" he demanded, out of breath. "Is something wrong? Was that wrong?"

"No! Sorry, I just . . . Sorry."

What was I doing? Why was he gone? Nothing made sense. I was crying. Already crying.

"Reed. Oh, God. I'm sorry. Are you okay?"

I held my stomach and stared at the pebbly carpeting of the stairwell through bleary eyes. Two minutes ago I'd been doubled over laughing. Now I was doubled over sobbing. I was losing my mind.

"No. I'm not," I cried.

"God, I shouldn't have done that. We shouldn't have—God, I'm sorry," he said, wrapping his arms around me and making me stand up. He pulled me against him, holding me. "Shhhhh. It's okay," he said in my ear. He moved my hair behind my shoulder and stroked it quickly, all the while holding me tightly with his other arm. "It's okay. It's going to be okay."

He said it over and over until I finally stopped crying. Until I almost started to believe it.

MORTIFIED

The next morning I woke up feeling like an idiot. Why could I not get my emotions under control? How long, exactly, would I be walking around like a ticking time bomb? I couldn't believe I had burst into tears in the middle of my first kiss with Josh. Maybe it hadn't been perfect, but he was still Josh. Sweet, funny, solid Josh. Josh, who could be a real boyfriend. Who was already a real friend. He didn't deserve to be treated like that.

Every time I thought about it, I actually shuddered in embarrassment. I was so mortified, I didn't even go to breakfast. I just sat in my room watching my e-mail inbox and eating Drake's coffee cakes, lifted from Kiran's closet and her faux box-of-shame. I was becoming a serial looter.

Around 10 a.m., I decided I'd waited long enough. The longer Taylor was MIA, the more my somewhat irrational concern started to feel rational. I typed up another e-mail.

To: taylor_bell@gmail.com

From: rbrennan391@aol.com

Subject: Please?

Taylor,

Seriously, getting freaked now. Just e-mail me back. Please. Thanks.

Reed

As soon as I hit send, my cell phone rang. After a long moment, during which I finally discerned that I wasn't in the midst of an *actual* heart attack, I reached for it. The sight of Josh's name on the caller ID made me cringe. I let it go to voice mail.

Ten seconds after it stopped ringing, it started again. Josh. Once more, I let the voice mail handle it. Once more, it started ringing again.

Finally I heaved a sigh and picked it up.

"Hey."

"So it's true. Third time *is* the charm."

I smirked.

"What's up?"

"I am. For a game of soccer," he said. "The question is, are you?"

"What?"

"Look out your window," Josh said.

I pushed myself away from Natasha's desk and crossed the room to the window. When I moved the curtain aside, there was Josh, on the path down below, grinning up at me with a soccer ball in the palm of his hand. He was wearing a dark-blue Easton hoodie and sweatpants. I had never seen anything so inviting.

"So . . . you don't think I'm a psycho?" I asked.

"No, I don't think you're a psycho," he said. "If anything, I'm the psycho. I think I was a little hyper last night and I . . . I didn't mean to be so forward."

A blush crept over my cheeks.

"Anyway, let's just forget about it. Can we do that?" he said.

Ouch. Did that mean he was ashamed of the kiss? That he never wanted it to happen again? Because I, for one, was willing to leave that door open. If we could take it a bit easier, that is.

"So . . . you want to play soccer," I said.

"I figure, what better way to get over last night than to let you kick my ass all over the field," Josh said. "Come on, Brennan. Show me what you got."

His grin, even from a few floors up, was infectious. But even more infectious was the realization that wherever we were headed, everything between us was going to be all right.

"I'll be right down."

ENTANGLED

Soccer was the perfect elixir. Not just the soccer, actually. The beautiful, clear, day. The view of the campus from the playing field. The cold air in my lungs. The exertion, the sweat, the burning in my legs. And, of course, the trash talking. Trash talking was always therapeutic.

"Oh! And she steals the ball *again!*" I shouted at Josh as I kicked the ball away from him, then chased after it. "I thought you were on the soccer team, Hollis. Your footwork is for crap!"

Josh tripped forward as he raced after me. He was fast, I'd give him that. Somehow he got in front of me and tried to block my path to the goal.

"I never said I was first string," he said, gasping for breath. "I kind of ride the bench, to be honest. Baseball's more my game."

"Ah. Well, that explains it. Cardio's not a priority when you're just standing on base all day, huh?" I stopped and put my foot atop the ball. Josh placed his hands on his hips and drew in a few deep breaths.

"Why're you stopping? You intimidated?" he asked. Rather, gasped.

I laughed. "No. Just hoping I don't need the defibrillator."

"Come on. Let's go," he said, wagging his hands at me weakly. "I'm getting the ball back."

I raised my eyebrows. "Are you really? Go ahead."

I crossed my arms over my chest and smirked. Josh looked at me. He looked at the ball. He looked at me again.

"Are you serious?"

"Yeah. I dare you to try to take it from me," I told him.

Josh shrugged and turned away. "Whatever. If you're not even gonna make it hard—"

Suddenly he whipped around again and kicked out his leg for the ball. My ninjalike reflexes, however, had long since switched on. I simply rolled my foot back, sliding the ball around my legs, where it came to rest at my other side. Josh tried to pull up and switch directions. Instead he tripped himself and slid forward. My eyes widened. His leg swept right toward mine and with a sudden swoop, I was going down, too. So much for those reflexes.

Suddenly I was lying crooked over Josh's side, face to the ground. We both turned to extricate ourselves, but instead our legs got hopelessly, awkwardly entangled. My heart started to pound.

"You really do fall a lot, huh?" I said, trying to turn over.

Josh turned on his side so that he was facing me. His chest was a mere inch from mine. He had a leaf stuck in his curls and a streak of brown and green across his chin.

"Actually, I did that on purpose," he said.

Gravity reversed itself as he leaned in to kiss me. Gently. Softly. Reverently. Sweetly. This was a real kiss. It was exciting but also comforting, like sinking into a soft pillow. It was as if we just fit. He touched my face with his fingertips and I rested my cheek on his bicep as I kissed him back. There were no thoughts of guilt or remorse or comparison in my mind. It was just Josh and the cold breeze and the scents of cut grass and fallen leaves. This felt like our real first kiss.

"Ahem!"

Josh and I sprang apart. I tried to scramble up but slipped on my heel and fell right back down on my ass. Hard. Standing not twenty yards away were three not-so-happy-looking men. Detective Hauer. Chief Sheridan. Dean Marcus.

"Perhaps I should have had a stricter schedule for those students whom the school was so kind as to host this weekend," Dean Marcus said. He looked cold. Cold and tired and annoyed and accusatory. Like he blamed us for the fact that he was cold and tired and annoyed.

"Sorry, sir," Josh said, pushing himself to his feet. He offered me both his hands and yanked me up from the ground. "Heat-of-the-moment thing. Won't happen again."

"It certainly will not," the dean said, walking toward us. The other two followed. Detective Hauer looked at me as if he was trying not to laugh, and I quickly cleared my throat and looked away. If he thought there was some kind of kinship between us, he was wrong. Especially now that I'd seen him following my friend in the dark for God only knew what reason. Until that was explained, we'd be sharing no amused glances. "I think the two of you should separate yourselves for the rest of the weekend. I'll make sure that both Mrs. Lattimer and Mr. Cross are aware of it," Dean Marcus said.

"Yes, sir," Josh replied.

"Yes, sir," I echoed.

"Mr. Hollis, Chief Sheridan and Detective Hauer would like a word," the dean said.

"More than a word, actually," the chief amended, sounding stern. "We have quite a bit to talk about."

Josh lost all color in his face. I stared at him, waiting for him to glance back, to show me that he was as confused as I was. He didn't. His eyes were locked on the chief.

"Why? Did something happen?" Josh asked. "What's wrong?"

"Nothing, Mr. Hollis. Nothing to be alarmed about," Detective Hauer said. "It's just now that your lead fell through we have a few more questions for you. We want to make sure we didn't miss anything."

"Normal procedure. You understand," the chief stated coolly. "You *were* the last person to see Thomas Pearson alive, so we're hoping there might be some details you've omitted—"

"I didn't omit anything," Josh said quickly.

All three men stared at him as if he'd just flipped them off. My stomach felt oddly hollow.

"Or perhaps some details you may have *forgotten*," Detective Hauer said.

"Oh. Sure. Right," Josh finally glanced over his shoulder at me, then wiped his palm on his sweats. "I guess I'll . . . see you later."

"I thought we already discussed that," the dean corrected.

"I'll see you soon," I told Josh firmly, hoping to convey some kind of solidarity and support in those four meaningless words. Josh was clearly freaked, and I hated that he had to go off with those men alone. It was so unfair that the focus was on him just because he'd been unlucky enough to share a room with Thomas. I wished there was something I could do to help him, protect him. Anything.

"Yeah. Soon," Josh said with a small smile, and I knew he got my message.

He kicked the soccer ball back to me as he walked off. The two policemen flanked him, and even though he was quite tall, he looked like a child between them, his head hanging. I glanced at Dean Marcus.

"I'll escort you back to Billings, Miss Brennan," he said sourly.

There had been a point in my career at Billings, however brief, when the dean had no idea who I was. What I wouldn't give to reclaim that anonymity.

A CALL

Mrs. Lattimer confined me to my room for the rest of the day. She came to get me at lunchtime and walked me over to the cafeteria. Josh was not there. She then walked me back. This was, of course, not necessary—I wasn't about to make a break for Hell Hall and bust in on Josh and the cops—but I kept my mouth shut. Lattimer smiled more during those walks than I had ever seen her smile before. Putting those hawklike qualities to good use made her happy, I suppose.

Alone in my room, I couldn't sit still. I couldn't stop thinking about Josh. Worrying about him. Wondering what they were asking him. What more could he possibly have to tell them? They had already interviewed him several times. It wasn't Josh's fault they couldn't do their jobs and figure out what had happened to Thomas. It was amazing how I had come to this school to study and better myself and ensure that I would never have to go back to Croton, Pennsylvania, after high school again, and instead I was spending the bulk of my time worrying about guys. Where had I gone wrong?

Just to compound my feelings of loneliness and confusion, Taylor still had not e-mailed me back. The more I checked my e-mail, the more disheartened I became. It looked like I was going to have to wait until she returned on Sunday night to talk to her, but I still wasn't quite ready to give up. I wrote another quick plea and sent it into the ether. Maybe she would message me to quit stalking her. At least it would be something.

Between the Josh situation and the Taylor disappearance, I was driving myself crazy with questions that couldn't possibly be answered, so I decided to force myself to study. Once I cracked open my books and got started. I was absorbed again. I had a lot to catch up on, and with each item I ticked off my list, I felt a distinct sense of accomplishment. What better way to keep my mind off Josh's troubles than to concentrate on thwarting my academic demise? It was definitely better than pacing the floor.

The sun started to go down early—as it did these days—and I flicked on my desk light. When my cell phone rang, it nearly startled all the major organs right out of me. I was surprised to see Noelle's name on the caller ID.

"Hello?" I said, pushing away from my desk.

"Hey, Reed. How's Siberia?"

"Fine," I said with a smirk. "How's New York?"

"It's New York," she said. "I spent half the day at Bergdorf's watching my mother try on slacks."

"How very glamorous," I said.

"At least I got a new purse out of the deal."

Like she needed one. She had about five hundred already, stuffed in every crevice of her room.

"So how's Thanksgiving at the caf? It's hard to believe anything actually goes on when we're not there."

I blinked, surprised. Was she really just calling me to chat? About me, of all things? She must have been really bored. Still, I was touched that she'd chosen to call me instead of . . . well, *anyone* else. I stood up and walked over to my bed, then settled back against the pillows for what might turn into my first-ever pointless phone conversation with a girlfriend. Yet another random way in which becoming a Billings Girl seemed to be paying off.

Maybe if I kept her on the phone long enough—got her guard down—I could ask her about Taylor. Find out what they had fought about, and whether or not Noelle had actually known Taylor was leaving early.

"It wasn't bad, actually, but today kind of sucked," I told her.

"Why? What happened?"

"The police dragged Josh off for more questioning," I replied. "They made it sound like they were back to square one with the investigation."

"And they think Josh knows something?" Noelle asked, sounding suddenly very alert.

"I don't know, maybe. They think he might have forgotten to tell them something that might help," I said, my heart turning over. "Actually, they sort of implied that they thought he might have purposely not told them something."

Silence. I expected a scoff or a laugh or some kind of reaction. All I got was silence.

"Noelle?"

"So what happened?" she asked.

"I have no idea. I haven't seen him all day," I replied. "God, what if they've had him holed up *all day* questioning him?"

"You seem more than a little concerned," Noelle said, suddenly sly.

I blushed and was happy she wasn't in the room to see it. Part of me would have loved to dish with a girlfriend about my new crush. But I already knew from my experience with Constance that this whole thing might not go over well. I didn't want to risk any negative feedback. Not when I still shivered every time I thought of our kiss.

"There's really nothing else to think about around here," I told her flatly. "I just hope he's okay."

"Don't worry. He'll be fine," Noelle said.

"Yeah, but—"

"Believe me. If anyone can handle an inquiry, it's Josh Hollis," Noelle said.

I froze. "What does that mean?"

Another beat of silence.

"Nothing. It's just Josh. You know Josh. He's the most mature person at Easton," Noelle said quickly. "He's more mature than most of the professors."

She wanted me to laugh, I could tell, but I couldn't. I couldn't shake the feeling she had meant something by her comment.

"Noelle—"

"Hang on." She covered the phone with her hand and I heard her shouting something, but it was muffled. Then, a moment later, she was back. "I've gotta go, Reed. We're late for drinks before the opera. It's kind of a family tradition. But I'll see you on Sunday."

"Wait a second."

"Don't read so much into every little thing, Reed. I was just talking," Noelle said in that patronizing tone that always made me feel like I was five. "You'll see Josh at dinner and everything will be fine."

I sighed. She was rushing and I knew I wasn't going to get anything else out of her. "I hope so."

"I have to go," Noelle said. "Later."

Then the line went dead.

My books sat on my desk, ready and waiting, but suddenly the very idea of getting up from my bed exhausted me. I hunkered down and decided to wait there until Lattimer sprang me for my next meal. Wait there and obsess.

INSIGHT

Noelle was right about one thing: I did see Josh at dinner. He walked in half an hour later than everyone else, with Mr. Cross, and he looked like roadkill. His skin was waxy, his face was drawn, and his curls were in desperate need of a hot-oil treatment.

Yes, that was the first thing I thought when I saw him. Apparently, pilfering things from Kiran's room was causing her worldview to rub off on me.

But in the next second, I felt an overwhelming, almost suffocating anger. That this was happening. That they were keeping us away from each other. That Josh was being put through hell. That nothing could just be normal.

I sat up straight and Josh glanced at me from the corner of his eye. In that one look, there was more anger and fear than I could even comprehend. He said a few words to Cross, they argued, and then Cross finally sighed and pressed his lips together in a disapproving manner. Then he nodded. Josh walked away from him so fast it was like he'd been pushed.

"Hey," I said, standing up as he approached.

I felt extremely conspicuous. My face was red. I could feel it trying to burn itself free. All I wanted to do was hug him, but every pair of eyes in the room was on us. Like we were suddenly the black sheep of the student body.

"Hey."

Dean Marcus glared at us as Mr. Cross came over and leaned toward his ear. My heart pounded with anger and trepidation. I focused on the anger and stared back at the dean.

Just try me.

He looked away.

Josh slumped into the chair across from mine and put his head in his hands. I deflated from my own exertion and sat down.

"Are you all right?" I whispered.

"No. Not really," Josh said. He dropped his arm down on the table and his watch smacked against the surface, making me jump. Up close, his eyes looked bloodshot and his pupils were huge. "They've been on my ass all day. They just keep making me go over that night over and over and over again, like they're waiting for me to crack or something."

"They don't think you had anything to do with it, do they?" I asked.

My heart was beating behind my eyes. They couldn't think that. It wasn't possible. Josh was the nicest, kindest, most decent person in this pit of egotistical, overprivileged psychosis they called Easton. If Hauer and Sheridan thought he had anything to do with

Thomas's death, they should seriously consider a change in profession, to something that required no intuition or insight into the human mind.

"No. I don't think so. I don't know." Josh pressed the heels of his hands into his eye sockets. I'd never seen him like this. "It's like they think that since I didn't tell them Thomas was dealing, there must be something else I didn't tell them. They just keep pressing and pressing and *pressing*." He said the last word through his teeth, gnashing them together so hard I thought they would shatter. He put his hands down again and I reached for one, holding his fingers in mine.

"That doesn't make any sense. Everyone in the student body knew Thomas was dealing and no one told on him," I said. Perhaps a bit of an exaggeration, but it was close to true. And I tend to exaggerate when I'm seething. "They should suspect every last one of us of lying now."

Josh blew out a sigh. "True. But they don't. They just suspect me."

I wanted to do something, but I had no idea what. I wanted to say something, but I had no clue what would help. I felt like I was being torn apart.

This was the definition of *unfair*. Josh was a good person. He was a good person who cared about his friends and tried to do the right thing, and here he was, upset and tortured and scared. And why? Because he had tried to protect the *wrong* friend. He had tried to protect a lying, scheming drug dealer.

"They have to stop," I heard myself say. "Sooner or later, they have to realize you don't know anything and they have to stop."

Josh crossed his arms on the table and lowered his chin to rest on them. With his fingertips, he grasped at the ends of his sweatshirt sleeves, pulling them up toward his palms and gathering himself in, like a little kid hiding from the cold. He looked so small. So scared. We stared at one another for a long moment, and I felt like I could hear our hearts pounding out a frantic rhythm together—an angry, confused, frantic rhythm.

"God, I hope so. I can't do this again." Josh was close to whimpering. "I really can't."

"I know."

I wanted to hit someone. Anyone.

Who was I kidding? I knew who I wanted to hit. Pummel. Beat with my fists until I was spent or he was dead, whichever came first. Only problem was, he was already six feet under.

"It's gonna be okay," I said, when nothing else coherent came to mind.

"I hope so." Josh shuddered slightly and squeezed my hand. "God, I really hope so."

In that moment, I hated Thomas Pearson. Dead or alive. I hated him.

THE ART OF DISTRACTION

I walked back into Billings on Sunday afternoon to a gaggle of voices and laughter and an occasional screech. I smiled as I closed the door behind me. The Billings Girls were back, and it was as if they hadn't seen each other in two months.

With a quick glance I noted that Taylor was not among the revelers in the lobby. I greeted the group, which included the Twin Cities, Rose, Cheyenne, and a few others, and made my way up to my room to drop my stuff. Noelle, Ariana, Kiran, and Natasha all turned to look at me when I opened the door. There was a brief moment of stunned silence, as if they were surprised to see me walking into my own room.

No Taylor. Everyone was there but her.

"Reed! Hey!"

Natasha broke away from the pack and hugged me. She was positively glowing. "How *are* you? How was your Thanksgiving?"

"It was . . . fine," I said. "How was yours?"

"Good," she said, lifting her shoulders. "Leanne and I hung out."

Ah. Hence the glow.

"Reed!" Kiran strode over in her tasteful shift dress and black heels and air-kissed each of my cheeks. She looked perfectly scrubbed, polished, buffed, and waxed and had adopted a new scent in her few days off—something flowery and soothing. Apparently, she was no longer irked over our last conversation. Unfortunately, I still was.

"How was it here without us?" Ariana asked as she hugged me lightly.

"Boring as sin, I assume?" Noelle put in.

"Like sin is ever boring," Kiran said.

Noelle smirked. "Touché."

"Okay, enough chitchat," Kiran said. "Let's do presents!"

"Presents?"

Kiran turned and picked up a big black shopping bag from the floor, dangling the rope handles from her thumb.

"For you," she announced. "For having to endure four days all alone at Easton."

I was stunned. Did these girls use any excuse they could find to buy stuff? And why did I get the idea that this was more of an apology/bribe?

"What is it?" I asked.

"Open it!" Kiran exclaimed.

"You didn't have to do this," I said, taking the bag from her. It was heavy. I slipped a big, sleek box out, and Natasha grabbed the bag before it could hit the floor. I laid the box down on my bed and lifted the lid. A clean, crisp scent hit me in the face as tissue paper fluttered. The scent of wealth. I carefully unfolded the paper and froze. Inside the box was a black cashmere-and-wool coat with a tufted silk lining. The tag had one word embroidered on it: DIOR.

Natasha whistled.

"Kiran—"

"Isn't it delicious?" she asked, ripping the coat out of the box. She held it up to herself and twirled. "When I saw it, I knew you had to have it. You cannot keep walking around in that ratty blue thing."

Ratty blue thing. As in, my brand-new Lands' End coat that my dad had bought for me. Part of me was offended, even as I agreed with her. My outerwear just did not measure up to the outerwear of the rest of the Billings Girls, nor to that of anyone else at Easton. Except, maybe, for Kiki, who insisted on walking around campus in a puffy black parka with fur around the hood that made her look like a sausage with hair. Although I had a feeling that was some kind of statement, whereas my blue coat said only one thing: middle class.

"Thanks, Kiran," I said as she handed the coat over. "I love it."

"My turn," Ariana announced.

They each had a present for me. A red silk scarf from Ariana, a pair of Coach sunglasses from Noelle, and from Natasha, a book: *The Lovely Bones.*

"You got her a book?" Noelle said, as if I was holding a pile of dog doo.

Natasha ignored her. "It helps. Trust me. You might think it's weird at first, but it's good."

I smiled. "Thanks. But you guys didn't have to do this. Really. I have no idea why you did."

"There's nothing to do in New York but shop," Noelle said.

Yeah, right.

"There are other things to do in Atlanta, but I've done them all," Ariana added with a small smile.

I placed all my booty down on the bed and hooked my thumbs in the back pockets of my jeans. I could no longer avoid asking the obvious.

"So, where's Taylor?" I asked.

They all looked at one another in a way that made the hair on my arms stand up. Like, *Do you want to tell her, or should I?* Finally, Ariana took the bullet.

"Reed, Taylor's not coming back to school."

My brain whirled. "What?"

"She's taking some time off," Ariana said. "She needs a bit of a *rest*."

She whispered the last word and scrunched up her nose, as if it displeased her to say it. I looked at Kiran, who was very involved in toying with my new scarf.

"What the hell does that mean?" I asked.

"God, Reed. What Ariana is trying to say is that Taylor snapped, okay?" Noelle said. "The pressure finally got to her and she lost it. It's not uncommon around here."

"Her parents checked her into a *facility*," Ariana whispered. Nose scrunch. "Nothing drastic. Just sort of a spa retreat thing. So she can regroup."

"Wait a minute, wait a minute. This doesn't make any sense," I said. "Taylor wasn't *under* any pressure. She doesn't even need to study and she gets straight A's. Taylor was *fine.*"

"Sorry. *Fine*?" Noelle said. "Have you not noticed the random waterworks and near breakdowns?"

I blinked. Okay. Girl had a point. But I had thought Taylor was just upset about Thomas's murder and that whole Harvard summer program thing. Was that really enough to push Easton's resident genius over the edge and into a "facility"?

"She's going to be fine," Kiran announced. "She just needs some time off. I bet she'll be back next semester."

"I'm sure she will be," Ariana said comfortingly.

"Well, can I talk to her?" I asked. "I've been trying to e-mail her."

"They usually cut you off from the outside world in these places. You know, so you can concentrate on getting better," Natasha told me. "She probably won't get back to you for a while."

Now I was seeing Taylor in a straitjacket, locked up in some padded cell, staring at the wall. This couldn't be right. She had seemed perfectly fine when she had walked out of here. How could things like this happen?

"A few weeks, at least," Noelle added.

"But . . . but I—"

"Look, Reed, Taylor is not coming back. Get used to it," Noelle said firmly. Then she smiled. "But *we're* here. And *I* vote for a change of subject!"

"Like how fabulous your new things are!" Kiran announced. She swung the Dior coat out and draped it over my shoulders, then stepped back to admire it. "Ah, yes. Now *that* is a coat."

I absently touched the luxurious fabric. Why were they being so blasé about this? Taylor was one of them—one of us. Or maybe I was overreacting. Maybe the whole thing really wasn't a big deal. Maybe this kind of thing really *did* happen all the time in their world. Judging by the way they were brushing it off, that seemed to be the general consensus.

Kiran grabbed me and pulled me in front of the full-length mirror. "Look at yourself!"

"Here!" Noelle said, handing over the glasses.

Kiran placed them on my face. Instantly, I was transformed into one of those waify fashionistas who were always stuck on the covers of *US Weekly* and *People*. I looked like a paparazzi-shy movie star.

"I've got it," Natasha said. She took Ariana's scarf and tied it around my head, covering most of my forehead and matting my hair down.

"Dear God, it's Sienna Miller," Kiran said.

"Please," I scoffed.

"You do look famous," Ariana said.

"If you walked through an airport right now, people would mob you for your autograph," Noelle said. "That's how famous you look."

These girls really seemed intent on steering us all away from thoughts of Taylor. And although I knew I wasn't going to be able to rid my mind of her completely, I also knew I would never get them to talk about her if they didn't want to. I took a deep breath and decided to let it go. For now.

"You know what she *really* needs? A signature scent," Kiran said.

"Really?"

I had never owned a bottle of perfume in my life. But somehow I liked the idea of everyone knowing that I, Reed Brennan, had a certain scent that was all mine. It seemed like something a sophisticated girl would have—a Billings Girl. It also seemed like something a guy might appreciate. Like Josh, for instance.

"Yes!" Ariana seemed thrilled at this idea. "Let's see what we have back in our room."

"Wouldn't it not be my signature scent if you guys are wearing it?" I asked, trying to get into the spirit of things.

"I have like ten bottles of crap I don't wear anymore," Noelle said, getting up. "Let's go."

My signature scent derived from ten bottles of crap? Sounded about right. I sighed with a smile as we all walked out the door. Drama and intrigue aside for the moment, it was good to have them home.

ACTUAL NORMAL

"We need to do something normal," Josh announced.

He sat down next to me at Sunday dinner, looking almost back to his old self. Apparently the police had decided not to stalk him today. Thus the regular-size pupils and lack of bunny-rabbit skittishness.

"Define normal," Kiran said, laying her *W* magazine aside.

"We could BASE jump off the chapel roof," Gage suggested.

I was about 99 percent sure he was serious.

"You cannot BASE jump off the chapel roof," Ariana told him.

From the look on Gage's face, you'd have thought she'd just insulted the size of his manhood. "Why not?"

"Because you'd impale yourself on Big Bubba before your chute even opened," I told him.

Natasha snorted as she continued to text away on her BlackBerry, which she'd been doing nonstop since her return. "Now that I would like to see."

Big Bubba was the nickname of this huge oak tree that stood

next to the chapel. It had a memorial stone at the base of its trunk indicating that it had been dedicated to the memory of Robert Robertson, class of 1935. At some point, long before I ever arrived at Easton, the tree had been christened Big Bubba. I guessed Bubba was Rob Robertson's nickname. You'd need a good nickname if your parents named you Rob Robertson.

"I mean actual normal," Josh said, pulling his seat closer to the table. "Not 'it could crack your head open' normal or 'I'll be vomiting in my friend's Chinese takeout by the end of it' normal."

"Hey! That happened *one time*!" Gage snapped.

Noelle and a few of the others laughed. Inside joke. They had a lot of those. So many that I was getting used to them.

"So, *boring* normal," Dash said.

"Actual normal," Josh confirmed with a nod.

"Sounds good to me," I said, smiling. "Actual normal is in short supply these days."

Josh's eyes sparkled when he looked at me. "Thank you."

I blushed. "You're welcome."

Josh reached out under the table and ran the knuckle of his index finger down the side hem of my jeans. Tingles everywhere. Suddenly all I could think about was kissing him again. Kissing him and not being interrupted by three stiff-as-a-boards bent on making our lives miserable. Or by, you know, my own blubbering breakdown. Somehow, from the look in Josh's eye, I knew he was thinking the same thing.

When? Where? For how long . . . ?

Okay, breathless.

When I looked up again, Noelle was staring at me. I froze for a second, startled, and when she didn't look away I became very interested in my vegetables. What was her problem with me *now*?

"So, what do you want to do?" Dash asked finally.

"I don't know. . . . Gage, would your dad have any movies yet?" Josh asked.

Everyone seemed to perk up at this idea.

"I haven't seen a new movie in ages," Ariana said wistfully. Whenever she was wistful, her southern accent was more pronounced.

"Nah. Those don't start rolling in till December," Gage replied.

"Gage's dad's in 'the business,' " Kiran explained to me with a couple of lazy air quotes. "He gets to vote for the Academy Awards, so he always gets all the new movies on DVD when they're still in the theater. So he can, you know, 'watch them.'" More air quotes.

"Oh. That would've been cool," I said, wondering exactly what Gage's father did in "the business." Had Gage ever met any celebrities? Somehow I doubted it. Because knowing Gage, if he'd been acquainted with any famous people, he'd have been dropping their names every time he took a breath.

Josh grazed my leg again and I warmed from my neck all the way up through my temples. I surreptitiously dropped my right hand down under the table and touched his fingers, stopping him. If he kept this up, I was going to melt. But instead of pulling away, he hooked his pinky through mine and held our hands on top of my thigh. I turned toward him and smiled goofily, resting my head on my left hand and letting my hair fall forward to hide my face from the rest of the table.

His grin was just as goofy as mine.

"I don't think we're capable of normal around here," Noelle announced rather loudly.

I flipped my hair back to look at her, my heart pounding as if I'd just been caught sleeping in class.

"I think you're shit out of luck, Hollis," she said, talking to him but staring right at me. "Around here, there's nothing but strange."

THE ART CEMETERY

The text message read MEET BY GRT RM. POST FNL BELL. J

That was it. That was all. And yet it was enough to keep me giddy all day long. My skin tingled with curiosity and trepidation as I approached Mitchell Hall, the large brick building at the center of campus, which housed the Great Room, where we'd held Thomas's funeral/drunken disaster, along with several other parlors and gathering spaces. I glanced over my shoulder before opening the huge glass door. Inside, the air was warm and still.

"Josh?" I whispered.

I took one step onto the paisley-patterned runner rug and heard a woman's voice.

"The holiday fund-raiser is one of the most important events of the year!"

Clipped footsteps approached from my right. My heart flew from my throat, pulling me with it down the hall and into the indentation around one of the many doors. The headmasters of yore glared down their noses at me from their gilded frames. The footsteps continued to approach.

"I will have nothing less than fresh holly and Douglas fir. Do not bring me one of those horrid Frasers like you did last year."

Ms. Lewis-Hanneman, Dean Marcus's assistant, strode right past me, talking into her cell phone. I saw my entire Easton career flash before my eyes. If she turned her head so much as an eyelash width, she'd spot me here, where I definitely was not supposed to be. Why was I always doing these things? Did some sadistic part of me *want* to go back to Croton?

"No . . . no! That is unacceptable! I believe I have been perfectly clear!"

Damn, that woman was wound tightly. She shoved open a door down the hallway and I glanced after her. I could see what Kiran had been talking about at Thomas's funeral. Ms. Lewis-Hanneman did have a nice body, probably the product of daily yogalates or something. And her dark-blond hair, back in a bun, gleamed under the recessed lighting. But had she really been carrying on an affair with Blake Pearson a couple years ago? Youngish or not, what kind of adult had sex with students?

There was a slam and she was gone. I was just about to breathe again when the door behind me opened and gravity took over. I fell backward, my stomach swooping skyward. Someone caught me in his arms.

"Reed Brennan. What, pray tell, are you doing falling into rooms where you do not belong?" Josh smiled down at me.

"You scared me to death!" I whisper-shouted, whacking his arm as I stood up. Every inch of my skin was throbbing now, unwilling to respond to the fact that I was out of danger. I straightened my Dior coat and glanced around the room. It was circular in shape, and I realized we must be inside one of the four rounded turrets that stood at each corner of the building. It was dimly lit, thanks to a few green-glass torch lamps, and heavy curtains all but covered the two tall windows. But the most striking features of the room were the paintings. Every last inch of wall space was crowded with paintings of all sizes: portraits, landscapes, abstracts, still lifes. There was barely an inch of wall visible between each work.

"What is this place?" I asked, stepping toward a beautiful canvas, all yellow and orange swirls.

"The art cemetery," Josh explained. "People are constantly donating artwork to the school, and they don't have nearly enough space to display it all, so most of it ends up here."

"Seriously? What a waste," I said.

"Well, some of it sees the light of day occasionally," Josh said. He hit a few keys on a laptop set up on a low table, which sat between two round-backed couches—the only furniture in the room. He turned the screen toward me. "They keep a list of who donated what. This way if, say, Sir Cornelius Mosley calls and says he's showing up for tea with the dean, they can whip out his prized Manet and hang it in the drawing room."

"Wow." I stepped past him and squinted at the long, long list. "So . . . why are we here?"

"Mr. Lindstrom's an old friend of my mother's, so he lets me help him with the collection. I keep the list up-to-date and make sure all the paintings go back where they're supposed to be, so I have keys to the room," Josh said, lifting a key ring out of his front pants pocket by his thumb.

"That's why *you're* here," I said, turning around to face him fully. "But why are *we* here?"

But I knew why we were here. It couldn't have been more obvious to the world. It was difficult to wrangle alone time at Easton. And an untrafficked room with a locked door in a remote corner of campus seemed almost too good to be true.

Josh smiled slowly. "I guess I was hoping it would impress you. Does it impress you?"

"Oh, *so* much. Really. The keeper of the art cemetery? Wow!" I joked, clasping my hands beneath my chin.

"Not that, you loser," Josh said, grabbing the flap on my coat and pulling me closer to him. "The fact that there is a room on campus to which I am one of only two people who have the key."

My heart pounded a sweet little beat as I wrapped my arms around his neck. "Now *that* is impressive."

"I thought so."

Josh grinned before leaning in to kiss me. Everything fluttered as his tongue searched mine, his hands cupping my face. We stood there for what felt like a very, very long time. Kissing, touching, gently searching. Slowly, he unbuttoned my coat, and I let the ridiculously expensive piece of couture hit the floor. I was very aware of the couch right next to us, and when my legs started to ache from standing in one place, I crooked at the knee and brought Josh down with me.

"We don't have to do anything," Josh said, breathless. His lips looked swollen and pink. He was trembling slightly. "I just wanted to see you. That's all."

"I know. I know," I said. I trusted Josh in that moment more than any guy I had ever touched lips with before. "Let's just . . . see what happens."

So we did. And everything that happened was sweet and pure and perfect.

CONGRUITY

What is Josh doing right now? Is he painting? Studying? Possibly sitting on his bed pretending to be reading, but instead daydreaming about me?

I looked down at my open history text and smiled to myself. I was descending into dorkdom over this guy—and it didn't even bother me. Especially since Natasha was downstairs in the lounge and not here to *catch* me spontaneously smiling.

I felt a pang of guilt oncoming and steeled myself for it, let Thomas's face pass before my mind's eye. At moments I wished there was something I could do to bring him back. I did. But at other moments I wished that I would have just stayed broken up with him before his disappearance. Then maybe my new crush wouldn't be overshadowed by guilt and sadness. I wished I could just be happy. I was human, after all.

The door to my room opened and I jumped. Noelle stepped inside and closed the door behind her.

"You scared the crap out of me," I said, my hand to my chest.

Noelle's nose wrinkled quickly. "I've always hated that phrase. I mean, just the visual." She shuddered. "That would be so unsanitary."

I rolled my eyes and pushed back into my pillows, setting the heavy book aside. "What's up?"

Obviously, something was up. She wouldn't have been here unless something was up.

"Not much."

Noelle walked over to my desk. She picked up a framed picture of me and my brother, put it back. Plucked the top off my one ceramic jewelry box, which held my four pairs of earrings, then placed it down. Slipped the novel Natasha had given me from atop a pile of books and flipped through it. I waited patiently as she pawed my things. It wasn't as if there was anything interesting for her to find.

"So, you and Hollis," she said finally.

A pleasant warmth spread through me at the mention of his name. I drew my legs in, knees to chin, and held them. Was she actually here for girl talk? First the Thanksgiving phone call and now this. Crazy.

"Okay, you got me," I said. "How did you know?"

"Have you not been paying attention? I know everything."

It always stunned me when she made statements like that. Who had that kind of ego? That kind of absolute certainty? I envied it to no end. She had moved on to my collection of classic novels on the shelf above my desk and was inspecting their well-worn spines. Not that I'd had a chance to crack any of my old favorites since arriving at Easton. Too much to do—studying, playing soccer, getting hazed, mourning boyfriends: My plate had been pretty full.

"Do you not approve?" I asked with a bit of a challenge.

Noelle raised one eyebrow at me. "Do you care?"

Of course I care. You know it. I know it. Who are we kidding?

I decided, however, to ignore the obvious and move on.

"He's so amazing, Noelle," I said. "He makes me forget all about Thomas. In fact, he makes me wonder what I was ever doing with Thomas."

"Something we all wondered."

I decided I'd ignore that as well.

"It's just that he's so good, you know?" I said. "He's like Thomas's polar opposite."

"I wouldn't go that far," Noelle said flatly.

My heart kind of halted. "What?"

Noelle sighed and moved over to my bed. She sat down near my feet and looked at me in that way that made me feel like I was the kindergartener and she was the teacher.

"Reed, there's something you should know about Hollis."

Oh. Dear. God. What now? Please tell me it's something good. Like he's the undercover heir to the British throne or his dad is the guy who came up with Google. Please tell me this warning will be along the lines of "You may have to get used to jetting around the globe and meeting loads of interesting people. Can you handle that?"

"He's only at Easton because he got kicked out of his old school. He used to go to St. James Prep in New Hampshire."

"Josh got kicked out of school? Please," I said.

"I'm serious, Reed. And it wasn't for anything normal like going on a bender or flunking out," Noelle told me. "There was this whole scandal involved."

I felt a tickle in the back of my throat. "What kind of scandal?"

Noelle blew out another sigh. I wasn't sure if she was having a hard time telling me this or if she was pausing for dramatic effect. If it was the latter, I didn't appreciate it.

"What, Noelle?" I prompted.

"His roommate died," she said.

All the air whooshed out of my lungs.

"Come on."

"Supposedly, he killed himself, but the details were all suspicious," she said. "Some people said that the suicide looked—"

"What?"

"That it looked staged."

I laughed. My temples started to throb. "Yeah, right."

"I'm not kidding, Reed. There was this huge investigation, and no one ever proved anything, but people suspected that the guy was actually . . . murdered."

A chill shot down my spine, but I ignored it. It was just that word. That god-awful word I could not seem to get away from. It was not the congruity of the situation. Because it wasn't even a situation. It was a lie.

"And—don't tell me—Josh was a suspect," I said wryly, holding up my hands.

She was not getting to me. She wasn't. My heart was *not* fluttering in a way that scared me.

"Well, apparently, rumors started flying that maybe he had something to do with it—"

"Noelle—"

"And then he, like, stopped taking his meds or something and went on this manic-schizo rampage that ended with him tearing apart the dean's office," she continued. "*That* will get you booted. Deans tend to like things tidy, you know."

"His *meds*?"

Noelle looked at me blankly. "You didn't know about his meds? Kid's like a walking pharmacy. He's on everything from Haldol to Ambien. It's a wonder he's not walking around drooling half the time."

At that moment I heard a snap. "Stop it, Noelle!" I was on my feet. I didn't even know how I got there. "Just stop it!"

"Reed—"

"No! This is some kind of joke, right? More hazing?" I said. I was shaking. My fingers trembled so violently I shoved them into my hair and held them against my skull.

"Reed, no."

I didn't understand. She wasn't actually saying what I thought she was saying.

"So . . . what, Noelle? What do you mean? Are you trying

to tell me that Josh *killed* this guy? Is that what you're saying?"

Noelle lifted her shoulders. "I'm just telling you what I know."

"Well, if he *killed* some guy, he wouldn't just be kicked out of school," I told her defiantly. "He would be in prison, right? Or do you people not go to prison?"

"Reed, calm down," she said. "I told you, they weren't able to prove—"

"No! I don't believe you! Why the hell are you doing this?" I blabbered. "Do you not want me to be happy for some reason? Do you just get off on seeing me miserable? Why are you lying to me?!"

"I'm not lying to you," Noelle said with an incredible calm. "I wouldn't lie to you."

"Right. Because you've never done it before," I said sarcastically.

Noelle stood up slowly. "Reed, I told you that was over. I told you that you could trust us now."

"Consider the source," I spat.

Noelle's eyes flashed. She was seething at that one, I could tell. But she took a deep breath and shook her hair back.

"Fine. I suppose I deserved that," she said finally. "If you don't believe me, research it yourself. It was all over the news. Or just ask the guy, see what he says. It's up to you."

"Fine! Maybe I will," I said.

"Fine." Noelle took a deep breath. "I think I'll go now."

"Good."

She turned slowly and walked to the door. She paused with her hand on the knob, gazing at me over one shoulder, her thick, lustrous hair tumbling down her back. She looked as beatific as a Renaissance angel. "I'm just trying to protect you, Reed. That's all."

SEARCH AND DESTROY

Josh's pen tap, tap, tapped against the tabletop as he scanned his essay for Spanish, reading it over for mistakes. He chewed on his bottom lip and tap, tap, tapped. The white collar of his rugby shirt had a small, nonspecific stain right near the left point. For some reason, I couldn't stop staring at it. *Tap. Tap. Tap, tap, tap*.

I could ask him, right? Just ask him. How long had he been going to Easton? Seemed like an innocent enough question. Why couldn't I just get myself to ask him?

Suddenly Josh looked up. "What?"

"Nothing."

I trained my eyes on my book quickly, but not before noticing that his pupils were really tiny today. Were they always changing size like that?

He slapped the paper down and I flinched. "This isn't making any sense. I need sugar." He pushed back from the table in the library and fished a dollar out of his messenger bag, then closed it back up. "Want anything?"

I smiled briefly. "No. I'm good."

"Be right back," he said distractedly.

He walked off and disappeared around the stacks. I stared at his bag. Every inch of me trembled. All I had to do was grab it. It would take all of five seconds to search the thing. I could do it, no problem. If I could stop trembling.

I glanced left. The Dreck boys who were always at the next table had their noses buried in their books. I could hear some angry guitar screaming from the earbuds of one of their iPods. They didn't even know the rest of the world existed, let alone that I did. No one would ever know.

I reached for the bag, then felt a sizzle of guilt and fear and pulled back. I hated Noelle for doing this to me. She'd turned me into a paranoid freakball. Pretty soon *I* was going to need some psychotropic meds, thanks to her. But now that she'd planted the seed, I couldn't not know. I glanced toward the stacks. No Josh. I grabbed his bag.

All I was going to find were vitamins. That was all he was taking. He had told me as much. I was going to open this bag and all I was going to find was some special one-a-day formulation for overprivileged teenage boys.

My heart was in my throat as my sweaty fingers ripped the flap open. I pawed through the contents. Books. Notebooks. Pens. A mushed, empty M&M's bag. Random crumbs. A crusty paint-brush. Dammit.

I swatted the flap closed again and ripped open the side

pocket. His cell phone clattered out onto the table, causing the non-iPod-sporting Dreck boy to shoot me a death-ray glare.

"What're you doing?" he demanded.

"Looking for a pen," I shot back.

"You *have* a pen." He was very cocky about this declaration.

Mind your own business, Detective Dork.

"I . . . need another color. It's a study-system thing."

He narrowed his eyes but went back to his work.

I almost cried. I was becoming a better liar by the day. But the close call was too much for me. I was just about to shove the phone back and give up when out slid a long, thin, plastic box with seven small compartments. Each was marked for a day of the week.

Every one of my vital organs was moving up my throat now. I opened today's compartment. There were five pills nestled inside nice and tight. So many they barely fit. If Josh had to take these every day, he hadn't yet taken today's dose. Today's *huge* dose. The pills were blue and orange and green and white, with various milligrams stamped on their surfaces. My heart stopped, then thumped so hard it hurt.

All kinds of drugs, from Haldol to Ambien.

Noelle had not been lying. At least not about this. Which begged the question, what else had she not lied about?

PROOF?

I rushed back to Billings like my shoes were a pair of ticking time bombs. I had just looked up Josh's various drugs in *The Pill Book* at the library—once I'd gotten over the shock that the Easton Academy library owned a copy of *The Pill Book*. I only even knew the drug-cyclopedia existed and how to use it because my mother had been referencing her battered copy for years. She kept it in her nightstand, and why not? It was her bible.

It turned out Josh was on medication for depression, anxiety, insomnia, and seizures. And now everything was as clear as daybreak to me. Of course Josh was medicated. Of course he was. He'd been acting strangely ever since Thomas's funeral. First, he hadn't reacted *at all* aside from at the very moment he heard the news. No tears. No sorrow. No nothing. Like he couldn't feel a thing, even when this horrific tragedy had happened. Then, a few weeks later, the even-tempered guy I knew had started to become way more emotionally askew. He'd gotten so tense with me when I'd missed his Boston trip. And then the manic state on

Thanksgiving. I'd thought he was nervous about potentially hooking up with me, but apparently he was just on an upswing. The pupils, the jitters, the quick mood changes, the sugar addiction all pointed back to some serious issues. Had his medication stopped working? Or had he missed a few doses? Who knew?

God, now that I thought about it, there were so many clues. I'd never seen Josh drink more than half a beer. He'd been the only sober soul at the Legacy. And what was that crack that Gage had made about him the other day? *Well, maybe it just hasn't been diagnosed.* Everyone knew about this. Everyone, as usual, but me.

The walls of Billings House shook from the force of my door slam. Natasha looked up from her desk at the ceiling as if she expected it to cave in.

"Reed! What is it?"

"I need to use your computer," I said.

I dropped everything on the floor. My bag, my new coat—all on the floor near my bed. I must have looked half out of my mind as I approached her, because she stumbled out of her seat without another word. The pocket of her fleecy sweats got caught on the arm of the chair and she tore herself free.

"What's the matter?" she asked me.

I sat down and double-clicked the Google icon. For someone in the midst of a panic attack, I was experiencing a pretty sharp clarity. I couldn't believe I was even able to function, let alone type. But I did. I typed *Joshua Hollis*.

Natasha was getting impatient. "What are you doing? You're Googling Josh?"

"What do you know about him?" I asked her. I clicked the search button.

"Not much. Just that his parents are world-renowned philanthropists," she said. "They've helped everyone from the homeless here to AIDS victims in Africa. Why?"

The Google results popped up. There were more than a million entries. I started a new search: *St. James Academy suicide*.

"Oh. Did you want to know what I *know* or what I've *heard*?"

Natasha's disapproving tone should have been patented. It could be recognized at even the faintest decibel level. So it was true. She'd heard about Josh's shady past as well. I glanced at her over my shoulder. Her arms were crossed over her chest, and she gazed down at me like she was all disappointed. This girl was going to make a great mother one day. Or a drill sergeant. I was about to apologize for being so very immature when she glanced at the computer screen and blinked. Her mouth dropped open slightly. My heart stuttered. When I looked back again it was all there in headline form.

ST. JAMES STUDENT IN SUICIDE SCANDAL

PRIVATE SCHOOL SUICIDE . . . OR IS IT?

POLICE SAY 'NOT ENOUGH EVIDENCE' IN

PRIVATE SCHOOL MURDER MYSTERY

"Oh my God."

There was a basketball hovering just behind my mouth. Natasha grabbed my desk chair and pulled it over. She nudged me aside and commandeered the mouse. Good thing. I wasn't sure of my motor functions at the moment.

She opened the first story and we scanned it together. Sophomore Connor Marklin. Dead of an apparent drug overdose. Bruises on his arms. Signs of a struggle. Alleged falling-out with roommate—a minor whose name has not been released. Police suspect foul play. Local authorities bring boy and parents in for questioning.

Then, in the next article: Suicide note ruled authentic. Parents of the deceased will not press charges. "We ask that you respect our family's privacy during this difficult time." Investigation closed.

I sat back in Natasha's chair. My body had been filled from head to toe with lead. I couldn't have moved if I'd tried.

"Everything she said was true."

"Everything who said?" Natasha asked.

"Noelle."

"Well, that would be a first."

"What if he did it, Natasha?" I said quickly. "What if he killed this guy?"

"First of all, I'd like to point out that Josh's name appears nowhere in these articles," she said.

"Yeah, because he's a minor," I replied.

"But Josh Hollis? Come on, Reed. You really think he's capable of something like that? You know him."

"I thought I did," I said. "But clearly . . ."

Suddenly, snippets of conversations with Josh started playing themselves out in my mind. Josh saying Thomas didn't appreciate me. How Thomas never thought about other people's feelings. Had he been trying all along to undermine Thomas? To *make* me hate him? To make himself—his thoughtful, considerate self—look like an angel in comparison? I remembered the look Josh had given me when I had first hooked up with Walt Whittaker in the woods. He had looked so angry, but I had thought he was angry on Thomas's behalf. Now I wondered . . . had Josh always liked me? Had he been manipulating me all along?

"He turned in Rick," I heard myself say.

"What?"

"That townie guy. It was Josh who turned him in. Josh who finally told the police that Thomas was dealing," I said, my mind rushing ahead. "Natasha, what if he just did that to deflect blame from himself. What if he—"

"Josh Hollis did not kill Thomas Pearson," Natasha said.

"How do you know that? The police questioned him all weekend long! And he was so freaked when they decided Rick was innocent. More freaked than anyone else," I told her. I felt like my heart was about to squeeze itself into oblivion.

"Even more so than the mob-mentality boys?" she asked.

"Why are you defending him?" I snapped.

"Because if you're right, then that means we've been eating lunch every day with a freaking murderer, that's why!" Natasha cried.

Her words hung in the silence. I suddenly felt as if the very walls were listening to us. Mocking us. Laughing at our paranoia.

"You're right," I said, rubbing my face with both hands. "You're right. There's no way. This is *Josh* we're talking about here."

"This proves nothing," Natasha said. "Nothing except that something horrible happened at St. James. Maybe Josh wasn't even this guy's roommate. There's no name. What're the chances it was actually him?"

Suddenly, I felt energized. "You're right," I said, turning for the door.

"Where're you going?" Natasha asked.

I stormed into the hallway, Natasha on my heels. "Someone has some explaining to do."

Noelle was just getting up from her desk when I walked into the room she shared with Ariana. Without knocking. She had a brown envelope in her hand. She froze and glanced at Ariana, who was fiddling with the lace on one of her throw pillows. The moment we arrived, she tossed it aside and stood.

"Reed!" Noelle said. "I was just coming to see—"

"Okay, so some guy named Connor died at St. James last year," I blurted. "But that doesn't prove anything. If Josh really was involved, why didn't you tell me before? You must have suspected something, right? With Thomas winding up dead too? Why didn't you tell me?"

"Reed, calm down," Ariana said.

"No! Don't tell me what to do!" I shouted. "Tell me what's going on!"

Noelle and I stared at each other. I could see her nostrils flare as she breathed. When she spoke, not a single muscle outside of her mouth moved.

"If we'd sat you down on your first day in Billings and told you about every single scandal that every one of the students at this school had been involved in, we would *still* be talking about it," she said through her teeth. "We didn't *tell* you because we didn't care. Until now. Until you made it necessary for us to care by hooking up with a psycho."

"He's not a psycho," I said automatically.

"I had a feeling you wouldn't believe me, after the way you treated me earlier," she said coolly. She flicked her eyes over me derisively. In that one moment, I felt like I had lost more ground than I had gained in the past two months. "So I got you this."

She held out the brown folder. It was thick and the flap was open.

"What is it?" I asked, too petrified to move.

"Just open it," she told me. "It's fairly self-explanatory."

I glanced at Natasha. She shrugged, at a loss. I grabbed the envelope, all high and mighty, and yanked out the document inside. It was about forty pages long. The Easton crest was stamped at the top of the first page. Typed across the center were Josh's name, his birth date, and the words *Dr. David Schwartz, Results of Psychiatric Evaluation. Status: Approved*. The pages fluttered in my hands.

"Not everyone has to go through a psych eval before being admitted to Easton," Noelle said. "You have to be a real . . . *special* case."

Natasha stepped up behind me to read over my shoulder. My vision blurring, I turned to the first page. The paragraphs were long and filled with jargon I did not understand, but certain phrases popped out at me.

"Seems to have accepted death of friend Connor Marklin . . . becomes truculent and withdrawn when asked to talk about the state in which roommate Connor was found and how it made him feel . . . refuses to discuss sessions in which he was questioned by police . . . grows agitated and borderline violent when asked if he had anything to do with death of Connor Marklin . . ."

I swallowed hard. This couldn't be right. It couldn't be real. There was just no way. My insides were crumbling in on themselves. I found myself sitting without knowing how I'd gotten there. Numb, I flipped a few pages and stopped on an entry from late August.

"Responding well to new medications . . . mood swings under control . . . expresses genuine excitement about prospect of starting at Easton and rooming with his friend, Thomas Pearson . . ."

"Oh my God." The document dropped from my hands.

"Where did you get this?" Natasha asked, bending to retrieve the evaluation. She slipped it back into its envelope and held it in both hands.

"Turns out doctor-patient confidentiality does not apply to everyone," Noelle said. "I'm sure the police have already memorized that particular document."

"We just want you to be careful, Reed. That's all," Ariana said, her southern accent softening her words. "It's not just a rumor. It's solid fact."

I trembled as I looked up at them. The three of them. Standing over me all concerned. Like *I* was a mental patient. My brain still refused to accept what I had just read. It felt like it was expanding, trying to fill my skull to keep me from fully processing the words.

"The only solid fact that I can see . . . is that Josh Hollis is really unlucky," I said, my voice surprisingly clear.

"Reed—"

"No. I am not going to sit here and let you try to twist everything," I said, standing. My hands were rock-solid fists at my sides. "I won't let you do this."

"What about the meds?" Noelle said. "How do you explain that?"

"So he's got a chemical imbalance. That's hardly gonna make headlines. Every other person I know is on Ritalin or Prozac."

"Yes, but he lied about it, didn't he?" Ariana said. "Why would he lie?"

"If you were on all that stuff, would *you* advertise it?" I demanded.

"I wouldn't," Natasha said.

Noelle and Ariana were silent and it buoyed me. I felt better. I did. My logic was actually logical. But it wasn't enough. I turned on my heel and walked out of the room.

"Where are you going?" Noelle shouted after me. "Reed! We need to talk about this."

It took every ounce of self-control I had in me, but I kept walking.

DEFIANCE

I needed to hear it from Josh. I needed him to tell me the story of what had happened to him last year. If I didn't hear it from his lips, I would always be wondering. And I couldn't have that uncertainty. Not again. I needed *something* to be certain.

I walked into my room and grabbed my cell phone from my bag.

"What are you doing?" Natasha asked, closing the door behind us.

"I'm calling him."

My palms were sweating and I could hardly breathe. I stuffed my left hand under my arm and held it there to keep it from quaking.

"Hey, Reed."

His voice filled me, as always, with warm fuzzies. Even as typed words like *withdrawn*, *agitated*, and *death* flitted through my mind.

"I need to talk to you," I said firmly.

"Are you okay?" he asked. See? Always concerned.

"I'm fine," I said. "I just need to talk to you. In person."

A moment of silence. "It's past hours."

"So we'll meet somewhere."

Natasha widened her eyes at me, but I turned my back on her.

"What's this about, Reed?" he asked.

"I'll tell you when I see you. Wherever," I told him. "We just have to do this. Now."

"Fine. The cemetery. I'll be there in fifteen minutes."

He hung up before I could say goodbye.

I tossed the phone on my bed and grabbed my coat and scarf. I might have been sweating, but it was frigid outside. I was practically trembling with anxiety. I just wanted to get this over with. Hopefully tomorrow everything could go back to normal.

Not that we had yet figured out what that was. I was starting to realize that the term *normal* was relative.

"You're sure about this?" Natasha asked me.

I checked my watch and buttoned the last button on my coat.

No, I'm not sure. But what else am I supposed to do?

"Yes. I'm sure. I'll . . . see you later."

Natasha sighed and I walked out into the hallway. "Normally," I would have been concerned about getting snagged by our housemother, but I knew that she actually didn't much care what any of us did as long as we could bribe her heavily enough. I didn't have the means for that kind of thing, but by now I knew plenty of people who would do it for me as a reflex. It was us against Lattimer, and we always had the upper hand.

I was two steps from the front door. I needed to plan out what I was going to say. How was I going to broach this? How did you ask someone why they'd been lying to you when the only reason you knew they'd been lying was because you had searched through their stuff when their back was turned. What was I *doing*?

"Reed."

I froze. As did my heart. It was Noelle.

"Where are you going?" she asked.

I turned around. She stood on the bottom step of the common stairs. I hadn't even heard her behind me.

"I'm going to meet Josh."

Her dark eyes were piercing. "Do you really think that's the best idea?"

She was too serene. Too placid. How did she do that?

"It's not true, Noelle," I told her, infusing my voice with certainty. "Josh could never hurt anyone."

"If you believe that, then why are you going to meet him?" she asked me. "What are you hoping to accomplish?"

"I . . . I just want to clear the air," I told her. "I want to be—"

I stopped myself. Noelle's full lips twisted into a smirk. "You want to be sure. Which means that you're not. You're not sure that this guy isn't a cold-blooded killer and yet you're going out, at night, to meet with him. Alone."

I could feel my heart pounding in every vein. I wanted to rip that smirk right off her face. She was messing with my mind again, her favorite pastime. I had no idea why she wanted me to believe that Josh was a dangerous psychotic, but she did. But this time I wasn't going to fall for it.

"I am sure," I told her.

"I don't appreciate this, Reed," she said. "I go through all that trouble to get you evidence, to prove to you that I would never lie to you—which, by the way, I should never have had to do—and this is how you repay me?" She crossed her arms over her chest and stared me down. "You're not going to go."

I pulled my hat down over my head, covering the tips of my ears. "Watch me."

Then I turned around and shoved the door open, blasting my way into the cold.

THE QUESTION

I stepped into the silence of Mitchell Hall and paused. The only light came from the tiny spotlights set into the ceiling, illuminating each of the ghostly headmasters. The place might as well have been a mausoleum, and for the first time since I'd walked righteously out of Billings, I considered turning back.

"Reed."

His voice echoed down the hall. He was nowhere and everywhere.

"Josh?"

My heart beat in my throat. Why was he hiding? There was nothing but the sound of the blood rushing in my ears. How could I have come here without telling a soul where I was going? What was I thinking?

Answer: I hadn't been thinking. I had been working on pure emotion, adrenaline, defiance. And now here I was. Alone.

"Josh, where are you?" I hated the fear in my voice, but it worked on Josh. He stepped into the hall at the far end, from the doorway to the art cemetery.

"Hi," I said.

Josh didn't smile.

Go home now. Get out of here.

"What are we doing here, Reed?" he asked.

I have no idea.

"I . . . I needed to talk to you."

"Then come over here and talk to me," he said.

I hesitated. There were a good twenty yards separating us. His face was half in shadow.

"Why don't you want to come over here?"

Okay. Clearly this was a mistake.

"Is it because of what you found in my bag this afternoon?"

I felt like I had been shoved from all sides.

"How did you—"

"Lucas told me." Josh slowly walked toward me. His footsteps were silent. Lucas? Ah, the Dreck boy. He'd done me a real solid. "Guys do talk, you know."

No wonder he was acting so strange. He knew I had searched through his bag. He was pissed. As he came closer, his fingers clenched and unclenched, clenched and unclenched, causing my throat to knot.

"Why didn't you tell me?" I said, staring at his hands.

"Tell you what?" Josh asked with a scoff. "That I'm on five different mood regulators? That if I wasn't, I wouldn't even be the person you, well, that you know and like? Why would I tell you that? So that you could think I was some freak?"

I stared at him. Who would he be without them? Did it matter?

"You do like me, don't you, Reed?" he asked. He was close enough that I could see his eyes now, and they were all hope.

"You know I do."

"So then what?" He reached for my hand. I flinched, and he looked like I'd just driven a dagger into his back. I felt guilty and sorry and sad all at once. "What's going on?" he asked.

Here it was. The moment of truth.

"Why are you at Easton, Josh?" I said quietly.

His face completely morphed. Everything went slack and his eyes swam. For a long, long moment he just stared at me like I'd betrayed him somehow. Finally, he turned away from me, shrouding himself in darkness.

"How did you find out?"

I took a breath. It hurt my lungs. "It doesn't matter. I just need to know. What happened last year?"

His back to me, Josh pressed the heels of his hands into his eyes. He let out a sort of low, strangled groan. It was insanely loud in the still hall. I flinched but didn't move.

"My roommate died, okay?" he said, turning his face slightly so that I could see his profile. "He killed himself and I found him and it sucked and I lost it."

"You lost it," I repeated.

"Yes!" he shouted.

I jumped. He whirled around and approached me. "Of course I lost it. Wouldn't you? You live with a guy for a year and a half and you think you know him. You *think* that if he was really depressed or something he would tell you. But no! No. He's walking around like he's king of the world and his shit's all in a row and you're going to Vail over Christmas with your families and everything's freaking fine, and then one day you come back from biology and he's there and he's dead and there's all this drool and blood from where he cracked his head when he fell and his eyes are all wide and you're the one who gets to find him!"

With one, swift step, Josh was right in my face. His eyes were wild. Wild and not the slightest bit familiar. I didn't move. My heart sent tiny little knives into my chest.

"But you don't believe that, do you?" he said, screwing his face up in indignation. He took a step forward and now I edged away. "You think I don't know what you're thinking? You think I don't know why we're here?"

With each word his voice grew louder, more strained. He kept coming. And now I was scared enough to contemplate running, but somehow he had positioned himself between me and the door.

"Josh . . . calm down."

I wanted him back. Wanted the Josh I knew. Not this crazy, spitting force of nature.

"Why should I calm down?" he blurted, placing one hand at the back of his head and flinging it away again. "I'm not an idiot, Reed."

"So what am I thinking?" I asked. I was stalling for time.

Trying to figure out how I could get past him. Wondering if he'd try to stop me.

"You're thinking, *Oh! Here's this guy on all these psycho drugs with two dead roommates in two years, both of whom may or may not have been murdered.* You're *thinking* I'm a *killer*!"

He barked the last word and it startled me enough that I tripped backward. Josh stood up straight and looked at me, his face turning to stone.

"You're afraid of me. Of *me*. God, how did this happen?" Josh covered his eyes again and took a deep, shaking breath. "I'm sorry. I'm sorry I yelled at you." His voice was suddenly pleading. "It's just been so much and I thought . . . I thought you trusted me. I wanted to tell you about last year. I was going to, that day in Boston. I knew Lynn would bring it up, and I figured it would be the perfect time to tell you everything, but then you weren't there and . . . and when you called me I was so scared you didn't trust me anymore and I . . . was right."

I took a deep breath and the tension inside me deflated ever so slightly. The violent outburst portion of tonight's program seemed to have passed.

"Can I ask you something?" I said.

Josh dropped his arms. "What?"

"Did you take your pills? Did you take them today?"

He sniffed indignantly. "No. I haven't taken them in a while."

I choked back a huge lump in my throat. "Why?"

"I was tired of being numb," he said, turning his palms

toward me. "My best friend died and I barely even felt it. What kind of person am I if I can't even get upset over the fact that my best friend was murdered?"

In that moment, even as I was still shaking from his rant, my heart went out to him. I would never understand what it felt like to be him. To have no control over how I felt. Somehow, I just wanted to hug him. He looked so desperate.

"I had to feel something," he said quietly.

There was a long moment of silence. All I could think about was how often I had wished for the ability to feel nothing. Over the past few weeks I must have wished it a thousand times.

"Maybe we should just go back," I said finally.

"No. We're not going back," he said. He was calm now. Perfectly calm. The intense swings of mood were more worrisome than anything else. "I'm not leaving here until you believe me."

"Josh—"

"Thomas was my best friend at this stupid school," Josh said. He stared into my eyes. Focused now. Intense. With each word, he took another step closer to me. "We've been *friends* since we were *kids*. He was the whole *reason* Easton even *took* me after what *happened* at St. James. I owed him *everything*. He *had* his *faults*, but I would never, *ever* hurt him."

Josh's jaw clenched as he spoke. Each word came out tighter, more biting. More violent.

"But you don't believe me, do you?" Josh asked, still advancing.

I backed toward the wall behind me. "Why don't you believe me, Reed? Tell me! Why don't you believe me?"

"Josh, please," I said. I pressed my back into the wall. Josh hovered over me.

"Tell me why!"

"It's . . . it's just, Noelle told me—"

"Noelle!" Josh laughed in freakish short bursts. "*Noelle* told you! Of course! We're all Noelle's little puppets, aren't we?" He laughed, holding his hand up and moving his fingers around. "First she tells me to turn Rick in and what do I do? I turn Rick in! Then when that doesn't work out, she decides to tell everyone I'm a serial killer! And you just go ahead and believe her! We're all such good little puppets!"

My heart pounded painfully in my chest. He was out of his mind. Totally and completely out of his mind.

"Well, not anymore!" Josh shouted, rounding on me again. He slammed his hand into the wall above my head and bore down on me until I shrank toward the floor. "Not me! I'm not gonna let her manipulate me anymore!"

"Josh, please. You're scaring me," I whimpered. "Please, stop."

Hovering above me, Josh's face changed. It was as if he was seeing me there for the first time. And in that split second he looked petrified, mortified, clear.

"Oh my God, Reed. I'm sorry. I'm—"

At that instant, I was suddenly blinded. A bright white light hit me directly in my eyes and I threw my hands up as tears rolled down my face from the pain.

"Josh Hollis! This is the police!" a commanding voice shouted. "Step back from the girl."

The glass door behind Josh squealed. I wrenched my eyes open. Josh's arms were up, shielding his face. He was a dark shadow against the flood of light.

"What?" he said.

"Step away from the girl!" the voice repeated.

Josh looked at me, baffled, and stepped away from me. Instantly three cops rushed in from all angles and converged on him. Another grabbed me and checked me over, asking if I was all right. Over and over again. Was I all right?

"Yeah . . . yeah, fine," I said. "What—"

"Joshua Hollis, you are under arrest."

"What!?" I blurted.

Josh stood perfectly still as an older man slapped handcuffs around his wrists. Detective Hauer was there, his expression grim as he watched the proceedings.

"For what?" he asked.

The cop grabbed Josh's arms and shoved him forward. "For the murder of Thomas Pearson."

NO

"What's going on?" I demanded. Shrill, out of control, seeing red. "Why are you arresting him? He didn't hurt me! He just needs help!"

"Reed, please. Calm down," Detective Hauer said.

"We should get her out of here. Take her into one of the parlors."

That was Dean Marcus. This was one infraction too many. He was going to expel me. There was no doubt in my mind. And I didn't even care. All I cared about was the fact that they were taking Josh away. That his face had completely shut down. That as they jostled him by us, he didn't even try to look at me.

"Josh—"

"I recommend you don't try talking to him just now," Detective Hauer said, standing between me and the mass of people that seemed to be all over Josh.

"Screw you."

"Miss Brennan!" the dean growled.

It just came out. Sorry. I'm from Bumblefuck, Pennsylvania, remember? Can't be responsible for my sense of decorum while my new boyfriend is being hauled off for murdering my last one.

The detective backed me up and I stared at the folds of his coat. The three of us stood in the center of the hallway as several police officers escorted Josh out the doors and into the cold. A couple more searched the floor with their flashlights, looking for God knows what.

"What were you two doing here, Reed?" the detective asked me.

I looked him dead in the eye, incensed. "You do not get to ask me questions. You told me once that you would keep me informed about the investigation. You promised me," I rambled. "Now I want you to tell me. Why are you arresting Josh? Did you find something? I don't understand."

The detective shook his head and turned away from me. "You need to calm down first."

"No!"

I grabbed the sleeve of his ever-present trench coat. He looked down at my hand, surprised, and shot me a look that said, *Do you really want to be doing that?* I did not let go.

"Tell. Me."

"Miss Brennan."

They seemed to be the only two words the dean could say.

The detective reached down and gently removed my fingers from his arm. He let my hand go and I crossed my arms over my chest, lifting my chin. They had nothing. I knew it. I knew they had nothing.

"We found the murder weapon, Reed," he said quietly.

My jaw clenched. I felt myself start to drift. A defense mechanism.

"What was it?" My voice was full.

"A baseball bat."

I blinked. My vision blurred entirely. A baseball bat. The violence that implied was too much for my brain to handle.

"Josh Hollis's baseball bat. With his fingerprints, and *only* his fingerprints, all over it."

One fat tear escaped and tumbled down my chin, dropping onto my sleeve.

"I'm sorry, Reed," Detective Hauer said. "You have no idea how sorry."

FIND THE PSYCHO

Dean Marcus walked me back to Billings. Noelle, Ariana, and Kiran all stood outside with their coats on, waiting for me. I didn't even feel relieved to see them. I was never going to feel anything ever again.

"We'll talk tomorrow," the dean said from behind me.

Tomorrow I would be going home. That was what he meant. Tomorrow this nightmare would be over and I would be returned to my previous nightmare.

"Reed."

Ariana stepped forward and hugged me. I didn't move. Didn't try to hug her back. She didn't seem to notice. When she pulled away, she gripped my upper arms with both hands and looked me in the eye.

"Are you all right?"

I stared at her. Looked past her to Noelle and Kiran. I walked past them all. Numb.

"I'm sorry, Reed."

I stopped short. Noelle had just apologized. Slowly, I turned.

"I'm the one who called the police. I couldn't let you be holed up in Mitchell Hall alone with that psycho."

I didn't ask how she knew where we were. She, as I was constantly being reminded, knew everything.

"Don't call him that," I said.

"Reed, he *is* a psycho," Kiran told me, stepping forward. "When Noelle called the police, they were already out looking for him. They had just found the murder weapon. If they hadn't gotten there in time—"

"Shut up," I said, my voice flat.

"Reed. I just saved your life," Noelle said.

I looked up from the ground and into her dark eyes. She really believed that. She believed Josh would have killed me if she hadn't made the call. Was she right? Was Josh the insane one around here? Or was it Noelle who was delusional? Delusional enough that she could make herself believe she was innocent? That she cared about other people. That she was above reproach. I glanced over at Ariana, at her cool, ice-blue eyes. At Kiran and her expectant, self-righteous stare. These were my friends. These were the people I had chosen. Who had chosen me.

"I told you, Reed," Noelle said, stepping forward. She reached up and flicked my hair behind my shoulder, smoothing it down. "I just wanted to protect you."

"I know," I said. "Thank you. I don't know what would have happened if you hadn't made that call."

It was what they wanted to hear. It was the only thing that would get me away from them.

Noelle's face finally broke into a smile. Mission accomplished. "You're welcome."

"I'm going to bed now."

My hand was on the front door at Billings when Noelle spoke again.

"I'll always be here for you, Reed. We all will. We're not going anywhere."

The wind whistled down from the trees, and a chill raced down my spine.

"Not ever."

NOT EVER

Natasha was not, as I had anticipated, waiting for me in our room to shower me with concern. Most likely she was up on the roof talking to Leanne, relating everything that had happened. Good. I felt like I needed to be alone. The lights were all out, but her computer screen glowed, casting an eerie blue sheen over everything. I sat down on the edge of my bed and stared.

A baseball bat. Josh's fingerprints. Hauer was sorry.

I couldn't stop thinking about what Josh had said just before the police arrived. That we were all Noelle's puppets. That she was the one who'd suggested Rick as a suspect. And he was right. Josh might have turned the guy in, but it had been Noelle who had planted the seed that day in the car. Did it mean anything, or was it just one more thing Josh had said to throw me off his scent?

Who was telling the truth? Was anyone? Did these people even know what truth was anymore, or had they just twisted its meaning to fit their needs like they did with everything else?

Natasha's computer let out a blip. I glared at it. It was impeding my downward spiral. Then I saw that an IM screen had popped up in the corner. Every inch of me started to throb.

It couldn't be. It couldn't. But I had to know.

I pushed myself up and walked slowly across the room. In the box was a screen name I didn't recognize.

Girl_with_a_Pearl: Reed?

My blood ran cold. As I watched, the computer bleeped again. Another message popped up.

Girl_with_a_Pearl: Reed? R U there?

I sat down in Natasha's chair. My mouth was clammy and sour. My fingers trembled.

Rbrennan391: who is this?

Girl_with_a_Pearl: prove u r Reed.

My heart stopped beating.

Rbrennan391: how?

Girl_with_a_Pearl: ur middle name, brother's name, dog's name. u have 10 seconds.

What the? How could I type that fast when I was about to quake to death?

Rbrennan391: Myra, Scott, Hershey. WHO IS THIS???

There was a long pause. I sat there, petrified, waiting for the computer to tell me that Girl_with_a_Pearl had logged off. Then, suddenly, the bleep.

Girl_with_a_Pearl: It's Taylor. Whatever they told you about me is not true. It's all lies, Reed. All of it. You have to believe me. . . .